BOOK TWO

Fangs, Claws, and Camouflage:

Witches' Brew

First Edition Design Publishing
Sarasota, Florida USA

Fangs, Claws, and Camouflage,
Book Two, Witches' Brew

Copyright ©2024 Frances Applequist

ISBN 978-1506-914-24-4 PBK
ISBN 978-1506-914-25-1 DIGITAL

LCCN 2016945064, BK2

July 2024

Published and Distributed by
First Edition Design Publishing, Inc.
P.O. Box 20217, Sarasota, FL 34276-3217
www.firsteditiondesignpublishing.com

Cover Image by: Deborah E Gordon

Library of Congress Cataloging-in-Publication Data
Applequist, Frances.
Fangs, Claws, and Camouflage: Witches' Brew / Frances Applequist
p. cm.
ISBN 978-1506-914-24-4 pbk, 978-1506-914-25-1 digital

1. FICTION / Fantasy / Paranormal. 2. / Thrillers / General. 3. / Zombies.

F2119

Author's Notes

Fangs, Claws, and Camouflage: Witches' Brew is the second novel in the planned *Fangs, Claws, and Camouflage* trilogy.

After fighting together to save the fictional town of Dohiyi in the first novel, *Fangs, Claws, and Camouflage: Zombie Problems,* the Marines and supernaturals sweep across the country to their assignment in the Florida Everglades. This breathtaking and complex environment has been infested with both zombies and the terrified refugees who fled the spreading pandemic in their neighborhoods.

Along with fictional locations, I have included Florida cities and towns in order to convey the scope of the damage done by the rotters—and by those trying to eradicate them.

I also capitalize military titles as a show of respect for the men and women in our armed forces.

Frances Applequist

ACKNOWLEDGEMENT

My full appreciation to...

...my cousin, Joe Pezza, for sharing his knowledge of firefighting.

...the *Write On! Cary* critique group for their encouragement and early feedback.

...Izzy Zarrillo, Glenn Hackney, and James Aura, for countless, individual brainstorming sessions on their novels and mine. Our shared love for the written word has been an agony and a blessing.

...My beta readers, Michelle Befano, Kim Ball, Mark Minisi, and Matthew Minisi for their honesty—so hard to hear, and harder to act upon.

These talented people are not responsible for any errors I may have in the published version, especially in my representation of the military, police, and firefighters who all have my appreciation and respect.

Preface

Fangs, Claws, and Camouflage: Witches' Brew

In the first novel in this trilogy, *Fangs, Claws, and Camouflage: Zombie Problems,* supernatural beings emerge from the shadows to help militaries around the world stop the spread of a pandemic zombie infection. In the rural U.S. town of Dohiyi, vampires and werewolves join a witch and a wizard to help Marines save what is left of the population. It is a test of the effectiveness and cohesion of a coalition comprised of beings who distrust each other.

In this second novel in the trilogy, the infection spreads into the deadly and beautiful Florida Everglades. Surviving military and supernaturals from Dohiyi are now tasked with clearing zombies from this natural habitat. Humanity does not make itself easy to save, and the tentative bonds between ancient enemies are tested. *Fangs, Claws, and Camouflage: Witches' Brew* is preceded by *Zombie Problems* and will be followed by *Sanctuaries.*

ONE YEAR AFTER DOHIYI

CHARACTERS LIST

THE MAGICALS

Alexandria:

Nineteen-year-old Alexandria is the daughter of the non-magical Martin O'Mallory and his wife, the witch, Keenu. Alexandria is also a seer. Her best friend is Missy. Alexandria has skin the color of honey, hazel eyes and dark, curly hair.

Keenu Kulae:

Keenu is petite and in her forties with dark brown skin, hazel eyes, and a wild array of long chocolate-brown curls. Soft-spoken, she is one of the most powerful witches in the United States and one of the thirteen in the International Counsel of Witches. She and her husband, Martin O'Mallory had three daughters: the youngest, the seer Alexandria, and the non-magical twins Johanna and Linett. Linet is killed in *Fangs, Claws, and Camouflage: Zombie Problems* and her family was never told everything. Keenu also has a non-magical brother, Ned—a police officer.

Hilanor:

Hilanor was born in Sweden in 1901. As a twenty-five-year-old expatriate living in Greece he met and fell in love with the vampire, Avianna Riardi. They spent decades together before the aging wizard asked her to leave him. They remain friends.

Wiccans:

Sybil is a wisp of a girl with a blond pixie haircut. Meg is only described as an older woman. Other wiccans are described and not named.

International Counsel of Witches:

- Keenu Kulae represents the United States of America and Canada
- Mariana Martinez, a bruja, represents Mexico and South America
- Amoya Gayle, a sòsyè, represents the Caribbean
- Bindi Tagari, a ngankayi, represents the Australian Aborigine and New Zealand
- Prisha Basak represents India, Pakistan, and Bangladesh
- Celeste Dominque represents Europe
- Brenna Elison, a noita, represents the Nordic regions
- Miri Petulengro, a vrajitoare, represents the world's gypsy population
- Sasha Petrov, a ved'ma, represents Russia, Kazakhstan, and the Koreas
- Ying Chang, a shulam, represents China, and Mongolia
- Natsumi Hayashi, a majo, represents Japan
- Esi Dubaku represents Africa
- Lamai Onruang, a penyihir, represents Southeast Asia, Indonesia, and the Philippines

THE VAMPIRES

Adam and Eve:	Two young teens were killed, turned, and renamed Adam and Eve by the vampire Kahl-maus. He wants them to be the first two in his child army, but every child they turned became insane and had to be destroyed.
Avianna Riardi;	Avianna was born and raised outside of Naples before there was an Italy. The German vampire, Kahl-maus, killed and turned her in 1210, when she was the defiant twenty-two-year-old daughter of an abusive alcoholic. Avianna has long, straight, black hair and intense green eyes. She speaks with a heavy Neapolitan accent and often slips into Italian phrasing. Her first and forever friendships are with the Japanese vampires, Isamu and Akio, and the wizard, Hilanor. Her true love, soulmate, and the only one she ever turned is Joseph Dante.

Henry Gull

Henry was killed and turned by an unnamed vampire during the American Civil War. He claims to have fought in every war since. At some point he took on classic film affectations and renamed himself Ulric Barda. Has come to the Everglades to fulfill his vendetta against Avianna.

Isamu and Akio:

Isamu and Akio Mizushima were eighteen-year-old samurai warriors when they were killed and turned by their sensei in 1588. Akio is taller with the fuller face. To preserve their existence, their samurai brotherhood imprisoned their sire. They have spent four hundred years seeking honor in one war after another—fifty of those years fighting alongside their friend and mentor, Avianna Riardi.

Joseph Dante:

The vampire, Kahl-maus killed Joseph in 1979. His sister, Gina's, best friend, the vampire Avianna, found him in time to turn him. Joseph was and is a surgeon with warm and intelligent hazel eyes, light-brown hair, and a welterweight's body.

Kahl-maus:

Thin, with blond hair, an angular face, and steel blue eyes, German born Kahl-maus (White Mouse) was given his name by his negligent human father. When Kahl was fifteen, he was killed and turned by an unnamed vampire who abandoned him. Kahl-maus's mind never developed past fifteen. When he killed and turned the willful Avianna Riardi, in 1210, the sire-bond failed and she remained defiant. Most of his attempts to turn children into vampires produced insane creatures that had to be destroyed, until he succeeded with the young teens he renamed Adam and Eve.

THE WEREWOLVES

Kristian Kristoffer: Kristian and his wife, Mary, were attacked and turned into white wolves by a brutal pack. When they were strong enough, the couple formed a pack of their own that lives in the Blue Ridge Mountains and does not hunt humans. Kristian is tall, muscular and Nordic, with shoulder-length white-blond hair, a square jaw, and steel-blue eyes.

Mary Kristoffer: Mary and her husband, Kristian, were turned into white wolves. As alphas, they formed a pack of their own that lives in the Blue Ridge Mountains and does not hunt humans. She has blond steaks in her chestnut waves, hazel eyes, and a lovely face.

Girl: The one the Marines nicknamed Girl had been a street urchin. She has dull blonde hair that never looks clean. She would be cute, if not for a perpetual scowl. Acting as though she never had a human name, she never gives her history or shares her story of becoming a brown werewolf.

Elderwolf: Nicknamed Elderwolf by the Marines, this werewolf is a rugged man in his late forties who looks systemically annoyed. Wolf blood helps his dark hair stay thick and wavy, with gray strands weaving through it. He had only told one person his real name. When anyone asks, the elder wolf says he lost his name with his humanity.

Jamaica Savann: Jamaica was turned into a powerful, black werewolf by a passenger in his cab. To keep his wife and son safe, he left them behind in Cincinnati. In human form, he is a tall and muscular man with charcoal skin and an eerie gold in his large, dark eyes. He has a straight nose, sculptured cheek bones, and sensual lips. He might still have a brother, Devan, in Jamaica.

Jaylan Savann: Jaylan is the young and human son of the werewolf, Jamaica. He has dark eyes, full, sculptured lips, and caramel coloring. After being abandoned by his father, the zombie pandemic breaks out and Jaylan's mother dies, leaving the boy to survive on the streets.

THE MARINES

James Nicci:
James is a thirty-seven-year old commanding officer in the Marines. He is tall and wiry with a long face capable of looking more serious than he feels. James has brown hair, olive complexion, and amber eyes. His family has a compound near the Uwharrie State Park in North Carolina.

John Ritt:
Ritt is a handsome man in his mid-twenties. He is a modest height and weight, but with cobalt blue eyes and light blond hair. He has stereotypical surfer-boy looks with Mensa-level intelligence and a Marine's courage.

Max Schwinn:
Max is six-foot, three-inches tall, with close-cropped blue-black hair and gray eyes. He is the by-product of a neurotic mother and a cheating father, but his role model is his Uncle Dean, a U.S. Senator. He has a thin arc of shrapnel scaring above and below his left eye Throughout the pandemic, and by choice, he remains Sergeant of First Squad.

Gregory Kowolski:
Kowolski is not tall, but he is muscle-bound with sandy hair and a mouth that turns downward, giving him a look of perpetual sadness. Kowolski is irreverent and gruff, and given to using expletives. His temperament keeps him the Sergeant of the Second Squad.

Barr Benwahr:
Benwahr is Sergeant of Fourth Squad, the perimeter guards on the front T-wall. Average height, His heavy lids half-covered green-gray eyes that sagged toward their outer corners. He had thick lashes, dark brows, and a long nose.

Marco Coraggio:
Marco has black hair, always a little longer than regulation, dark eyes, and perfect features. His loose grasp of military rules, crooked smile, and brand of justice holds have kept him a Lance Corporal, but he is also one of Sergeant Schwinn's best Marksmen.

Creole Vanyan: At birth, his mother named Creole in honor of her heritage. On his seventeenth birthday, his ex-con father caught him helping a gang boost cars and made him chose between the army and prison. Tall, thin, and chatty with a heavy southern accent, he has remained a Lance Corporal and one of Schwinn's best Marksmen.

THE CIVILIANS:

Missy Senko: Alexandria's college friend and journalism classmate. Missy is the writer while Alexandria is the photographer. Pretty and slender Missy has her father's dark brown eyes, and her mother's golden waves and fair complexion. She typically dresses in a tank top, navy boot-cut jeans, a blue denim jacket, sneakers, and a cowboy hat.

Gabriel: Gabriel is the old and scrawny guide boat captain with a thick head of hair and a thicker southern accent.

Caleb and Longset: Caleb is a bald and gruff man and one of Gabriel's crewman. Longset is a heavy man and the other crewman for Gabriel.

Shea O'Cleary: Teenage Shea O'Cleary is a militia fighter from Dohiyi who comes to the 'glades to fight. She is in her late teens with a brother living with Dohiyi's Sheriff and the family's adopted Great Dane named Blue.

TABLE OF CONTENTS

Chapter 1

The Marines Have Landed

On the edge of the Everglades National Park, the Marines commandeered an abandoned visitors center. This Everglades base, under the command of Second Lieutenant John Ritt, would be home for the Marine squads and supernaturals tasked with clearing zombies out of the park.

Facing the street, and along half of each side, Marine contractors constructed a nine-foot-high, steel-reinforced concrete T-Wall. Spaced along the walls, Sergeant Barr Benwahr's Fourth Squad wore hazmat suits and fired on the zombies within range. They counted on their gunfire to draw more biters from civilian neighborhoods.

A female voice from within a hazmat suit yelled, "I hate killing the young ones."

The Marine to her right fired at an elderly man in a lab coat who had just begun to rot.

The woman grumbled, "Yeah. I know. Shoot now, care later."

A gruff, older voice came from the suit to her left: "In Dohiyi, one of them Japanese vampires said that we're freeing their spirits. Since then, I've wanted every shot to yank one of 'em from Hell for a quick trip to Heaven."

The woman fired, and then mumbled to herself, "That helps."

On the unwalled sections of camp, the raised walkway spanned shallow beds of saltmarsh grasses, reeds, and sedges. In the center of camp, contractors retrofitted existing buildings to create a chapel, commissary, CSH (field hospital), communications center, and barbershop. To house the fighters, they raised tents on platforms, supported by pylons. Marines added two water towers and the camp drew power from the state's power grid.

Ritt and Benwahr strode along the rear walkway that bordered a canal. Ritt's cobalt blue eyes and surfer-boy looks contrasted with the shorter and swarthy Benwahr. Where they stopped, they could watch whirligig beetles. The beetles, with their eyes divided both above and below the surface, swam in rapid circles and formed air bubbles for their dives. At night, the adults would fly in search of another pond.

Second Lieutenant Ritt hid his light blond hair under his helmet. Sergeant Benwahr, shorter but well-built, had a complexion almost as dark as his hair. His green-gray eyes never twinkled and he seldom smiled.

Ritt spoke first: "Make no mistake, Sergeant. The Everglades is a player in our fight to clear it. Sometimes it'll help us . . . and sometimes it'll fight us."

A heartbeat later, both men aimed their guns at movement in the tree above them. Ritt yelled, "Drop your weapons to the walkway and come down, now! I won't count to three."

A female voice called down, "Don't shoot! It's Shea." Shouldering her rifle, the girl pulled off her oversized baseball cap and her red waves fell over her shoulders.

Ritt yelled, "Shea? From Dohiyi?"

"Yes, sir."

Ritt ordered, "Comet down here."

While she clambered toward the walkway, he radioed for a guard.

Eighteen-year-old Shea O'Cleary, a head shorter than Ritt with a new scar on her face, shoved her unruly red hair back under her baseball cap.

As the guard moved in next to her, Ritt demanded, "Explain."

"I fought zombies with different militias from North Carolina to Florida. Then I came here."

"Why?"

Her face paled and she sputtered, "Because they aren't you—your people, I mean."

"Don't you still have a brother at home?"

Shea's voice quivered as she insisted, "My brother is safer with the sheriff's family. He loves them and he loves Blue—that Great Dane the sheriff rescued. Lieutenant, I can't sit out the war, but I need to be with the people I trust the most."

2

Ritt pressed his lips together to keep from smiling at her gumption. Then he asked, "You're what? Sixteen?"

"Eighteen, sir, and you already know I can fight."

"You shot zombies from a second-floor window. That means you can shoot, but it doesn't mean you can fight."

She flushed and protested, "I spent two years defending Dohiyi before your Marines came and blew things up. I fought and I survived, and I'll keep doing it with or without you!"

"It won't be with us. Guard, take Miss Shea over to the guide boat captains. They can always use a good shot."

"Yes, sir."

Shea began to protest.

Ritt cut her off with, "Shoot from the guide boats or leave camp."

Shea straightened her shoulders. After a dramatic pause, she followed the guard.

When she was too far to hear, Benwahr asked, "You trust her?"

"She was with the militia firing from a building on the other side of the park from us. Her commander reported that, while she was with them, zombies took her parents. Her little sister walked into her sites already bitten."

"Shit."

"Following tradition for that militia, she put down her own sister."

Benwahr mused, "Pretty girl."

"The zombies won't care. Now, we have a meeting to attend."

The two men made their way to the command tent and entered without announcing themselves.

Inside, Greg Kowolski removed his helmet and ruffled his sand-colored hair. The muscular Marine, who still led Second Squad, complained, "Really? So, we fought from Dohiyi in the Blue Ridge Mountains down through the small towns of South Carolina; along Georgia's Ochlockonee River; and along the St. John's River—just to end up in a swamp? Our nickname's changed from Number One to River Rats to Swamp Bunnies. Who in Hell are we trying to save here?"

Small but athletic Prem Kunchai, the oldest of Ritt's Sergeants, had become the new leader of Third Squad—the one Ritt led in Dohiyi. He shrugged and said, "Small towns, rivers, swamps: we're good at it."

Kowolski grunted, "This ain't a small town. This ain't any town. This is just gators and mosquitos."

Max Schwinn, leaning back in his chair, had the same square face and thick brows as his famous uncle. The senator had wanted his nephew moved to a desk job. Instead, Max passed on the promotion to keep leading First Squad. Noticing the Lieutenant, he jumped to his feet to salute.

The other men did the same.

Ritt put them at ease. He walked over to a map on the table and said, "I have the most recent percentages."

The Marines took seats to listen.

"Worst news first. In the biggest cities, healthy people kept mixing with infected ones, causing a sea of zombies. Police, National Guard, and firefighters ended up infected. When New York, Jersey City, Chicago, and Newark lost 60% of their populations, the military walled them off. They gave healthy survivors time to evacuate then firebombed the buildings."

A heavy silence blanketed the room.

Ritt pushed his hand through his short hair and grumbled, "Nationwide we've lost 35% of our police, 24% of our National Guard, and 20% of our firefighters. We've also lost 65% percent of the reporters and camera operators, which shut down most papers and news stations." He tapped the map and said, "There's a little good news. Towns with military bases, military schools, National Guard bases, or militias held their civilian losses to 25%. In cities like Chicago, L.A. Camden, Detroit street gangs are helping the police hold civilian losses at 30%." He faced Kowolski and added, "As far as our deployments are concerned, Sergeant Kowolski with the Ellis Island misspelling—we go where we're fucking told to go. Right?"

"Yes, sir."

"Good. The last thing this country needs is to leave zombies in remote pockets who can restart the whole damn thing after we think we've won. And we will win, won't we Sergeant?"

"Yes sir."

Schwinn interrupted to ask, "The samurai vampires have stayed with us most of the time, and the werewolves show up when we need them. But will we be seeing Avianna again?"

4

"I don't know, but we need walkway roofs and sun-blocking screens for the samurai brothers, so they can walk around camp during the day. I'm told the witch will be here, and that'll be different."

Kunchai blurted out, "Sounds unofficial."

"They aren't military, Kunchai. They can't be ordered."

Kowolski interjected, "Well, that pretty vamp and her boy toy were a lot of help in the North Carolina fighting but they haven't been with us since."

"She'll come or not. We do our jobs with or without them. For now, you're dismissed."

After his Sergeants left, Ritt walked over to the railing above the guide boats.

On the platform below, Shea was yelling at a scrawny, older man: "I counted heads, and you're missing a man. You need another shooter, and I'm really good."

"How good?" he asked.

"Two years knifing and shooting rotters in Dohiyi, North Carolina."

A younger man in another boat yelled, "We heard all about Dohiyi. You lost thirty percent of the town before the Marines saved your asses."

Shea flinched and a red curl dropped from under her cap. She shouted back, "If our militia hadn't fought so hard, zombies would have wiped out the town long before the Marines arrived!"

The other guides stopped loading their boats to observe the spat. The older man, Gabriel, pointed south and said, "Now, you look over there— 'bout two hundred yards. See them small flowers covering a vanilla vine? Shoot any of those purple flowers." Then he added, "Time it with the perimeter fire, so we don't draw biters to us."

Shea positioned her rifle and slowed her heart. Her hands, arms, shoulders, and back became one with her weapon. She waited for perimeter fire, and then made a shot that turned a flower into dust.

A young guide, peering through binoculars, smiled, while others whooped. Someone yelled, "Hot damn."

The heavyset captain said, "Okay, Little One. Gabriel already has Caleb and Longset, and the other boats are full, so you come with me. I'm Bobby." He pointed toward the dock and added, "Grab that blue duffle and toss it to me."

Shea told herself, without believing it, that she did not need to be with the Marines to make a difference.

Above them, Ritt nodded and made his way to the commissary.

Chapter 2

Vengeance and Duty

Hours away from the Marine base, Joseph and Avianna slept through their daylight hours. Slender, pale, raven-haired Avianna drifted through her dream until a figure emerged from its darkness. With skin the color of dark chocolate and long brown curls, the intruder hovered as though underwater.

Avianna's green eyes widened as she queried, "Keenu?" She waited a moment before asking, "Am I dreaming you, or are you dreaming me?"

No answer.

The eight-hundred-year-old vampire, who still appeared twenty-two, teased, "You do know that I own a phone?"

With a hardened voice, Keenu retorted, "I'm not laughing."

"What do you want?"

"Tell me who killed my daughter."

Avianna remembered Linett's screams and flinched. Images of zombies tearing her friend's flesh—releasing a torrent of blood—triggered the vampire's arousal and self-disdain. She had no words of consolation for the girl's mother.

"Avianna, did you kill my daughter?"

Lost in the past, Avianna did not hear the question.

Keenu yelled, "Was it you?"

Wrenching herself forward, the vampire whispered, "No."

"Who killed her and made her a vampire?"

Remembering her father's abuse, Avianna said, "I understand rage." Remembering how she killed him, she said, "I understand vengeance— but, the year before the zombie outbreak, Joseph and I found Linett already killed, turned, frightened, and dirty." Holding back the word, hungry, Avianna finished with, "your daughter came with us.

"Please believe that we helped her find moments of joy. We swam under the stars in the Mediterranean and in a lake in the Krubera cave. We attended concerts in the world's most magnificent opera houses. I arranged for her to play her violin on stage at the Royal Albert Hall in London." The mother's tears stopped the vampire.

"Who sired her?"

"We do not know. All we know is that her sire taught her to—," biting back the words, 'kill and feed,' Avianna said, "—survive."

The witch's hazel eyes narrowed. With a long, low moan she blended into the darkness until nothing remained.

Avianna rose from the depths of the dream into her cool cotton sheets. Under the mattress a three-by-six-foot zippered plastic bag contained the thin layer of Neapolitan soil that anchored the vampire to the world. She smiled. The invention of plastic bags made it unnecessary to drag coffins from country to country.

Fully awake, Avianna's vampiric vision allowed her to see through the darkened room at its sky-blue walls and white moldings. She stood and smoothed the red satin nightgown over her slender hips. The beige and white stone tiles did not chill her bare feet. Having evaded final death for over eight-hundred years, the vampire embraced every sensory detail of existence.

"Avianna?" Joseph asked in a sleepy voice, "We have to talk."

The vampire gazed back at the man she loved. His light brown hair lay over his pillow. One muscular arm rested on the sheet. Avianna's eyes traced the lines of his legs under the thin fabric, but a resurging memory of Linett's final agony killed the vampire's desires. She answered, "I am thirsty and going to the kitchen to warm a blood blank donation—so distasteful, but preferable to drinking a fellow warrior. Do you want to join me?"

"Drink animal blood with me—at least until the pandemic is over and you can trust drinking people again."

She wrinkled her nose and shook her head.

He slipped out of bed and repeated, "We have to talk."

"It is almost dark. Soon we will be able to swim in our indoor pool and see the stars through its glass roof. It is the reason I bought this house. Join me."

"Avianna, I am not going to stop saying that we have to talk."

She walked toward the door, murmuring, "The samurai taught me a great deal during our stay in Thessaly, but I need more practice. Would you like to spar with me?"

"You rode with Genghis Khan and, later, with his grandson Kublai Khan. You didn't need the twins to train you in Thessaly, and you don't need practice now."

Her back stiffened as she explained, "Genghis and Kublai Kahn fought during the day, while I thinned their enemy's ranks at night—so, in Dohiyi I fought in my first large battle—and I failed." Then she snaped, "I failed to save Linett, and the zombies almost had you."

"Dohiyi gave me more experience. You won't come close to losing me again."

Her voice rose as she continued, "What about your helping with the research at the Key West Lab? Helping to find a cure is more important than adding one more fighter among so many."

Guttural sounds outside, pulled Avianna back into the room. With her nightgown swirling around her legs, she moved the sun-blocking shades, opened the French doors, and stepped out into the twilight. Standing on the wide balcony, she stared past her gardens and across the channel. Her extraordinary hearing placed a horde of zombies over a mile away. She strode back through the bedroom, and Joseph followed her down the hall.

"*Sangue.*"

He recognized the word, blood, and followed her into the birchwood and black granite kitchen.

There, she used an in-line fluid warming machine to warm a blood bank donation. Then she poured the blood into a crystal goblet. Crinkling her nose again, she carried the glass out to the salted pool and stared up at the emerging stars. Pulling up her gown, she sat on the edge of the pool skirting, and eased her legs into the water. Shaking her head, she swung her legs back out of the pool.

Joseph, who had remained in the doorway, explained, "There are now enough researchers at the lab, for me to rejoin Nicci."

"That *impotente* animal blood you drink does not make you as strong or fast as you should be, and I am too selfish to lose you. So, *Stallo*."

"*Stallo* means stalemate, right? But this is not a stalemate, Avianna. There are different considerations here. Because I've only been a vampire for thirty-five years, I still have more substance than you. No matter what I drink, I will not be as fast or as strong as you are—but I'm faster and stronger than a human so I can help the Marines."

"I need more training."

Joseph gasped, "That might be the first time you've lied to me!" Calming himself, he said, "You stalled in Thessaly with the excuse that you needed more training, and even pulled the samurai over there to help you! When they saw how well you can still fight, they left to rejoin Nicci. Then you made the excuse that I needed to come here: to the lab to help find a cure." His pale face tinted pink as he added, "All that time, Nicci's Marines and the other supernaturals kept fighting, from North Carolina to Florida. Without us there, they lost more people. Now they're in the Everglades, and I want to help."

Avianna stood and crossed the distance between them, saying, "Your transmutations are terrible, your ability to mesmerize is limited, and you are weaker and slower on animal blood than you would be on human blood. Going into the Everglades to kill zombies might end you."

"I'm rejoining the Marines tomorrow: with or without you."

Moving into his arms, she purred, "Make love to me. Tomorrow will come soon enough."

He laughed and said, "You're incorrigible, but I do love you." He kissed her, tasting human blood on her lips. Holding her tighter, kissing her harder, his awakened hunger fueled his lust.

They ended their disagreement in the pool, naked in each other's arms. They both understood that he would rejoin the Marines and she would go with him. Giving no more thought to the risks ahead, they made the hours until sunrise unforgettable.

The next day, as Joseph handed his research to his colleagues, Avianna leaned against their black Bentley in the parking garage below. Her heightened senses detected rodents sifting through trash in the dark corners, piping creaking above her, and electricity crackling within the wiring. The cement under her feet reeked of car oil and beer, and the walls around her stunk of cigarette smoke and perfumes. Outside, bats—real ones, not vampires—chittered in the oleander and jacaranda trees that surrounded the building.

A skin-crawling awareness of another vampire hit her. She stood away from the car and pushed her dark hair behind her. She smoothed the hipline of her white summer shift and waited.

Tall and lean, with an angular face, the stranger was dressed like a Hollywood Dracula. He stopped six feet away and asked, "Do you remember me? We met two centuries ago. My name is Ulric Barda."

Avianna's eyes glowed in the dark. Her accent emphasized her Neapolitan birthright. "*Sì e no.*" she teased, "I know you are newer than you say, that your real name is Henry Gull, and that I met you only a century ago. Even then, you had trouble with the truth."

"Are you pretending that accent of yours is real?"

"Although I have traveled the world, Naples is the place of my birth. Throughout my eight centuries, I have returned to that region. Unlike you, Henry, I am…" she searched for the English word, "…authentic."

"Ulric," he corrected, "and I have come about a creation of mine—Linett."

Her voice softened as she said, "Ah. You are her sire."

Blue veins bulged beneath his translucent skin. His teeth lengthened and his eyes reddened. Stepping forward, he snarled, "You took her into a battle she couldn't survive; then you did not save her!"

Avianna's skin and teeth remained human. She did not step forward. Keeping her voice low, she asserted, "And you murdered her, made her a vampire, and only taught her to kill. You gave her a meager and miserable existence that she fled."

"I protected her. You, with all your self-serving speeches, did not!"

Avianna instantly closed the gap between them.

He backed away.

A smile pulled at the corners of her ruby lips as she asked, "What do you want?"

"Vengeance for my daughter."

An image of Keenu flashed through the vampire's mind. With a chilling smile, she said, "You are not alone, but ending the zombie pandemic is more important than any of your vengeances."

"I know you fight alongside the Marines. I'll help."

"Your help is *non e necessasario.*"

"All help is necessary. I have my anger and—if you cared about Linett—you have your guilt. Both must be purged, but no one will be safe until the zombies are gone. We'll fight alongside each other; then we'll fight each other."

She raised her head to listen then added, "Joseph is nearing us. Do not share your intentions with him. He must face the zombies unburdened." As her lover approached, she added, "One more thing: fight at Joseph's side. If he perishes, I will never give you your fight."

Before Joseph reached them, Ulric whispered, "Agreed."

Avianna nodded and said, "*Concordato.*"

Emerging from the shadows, the shorter, sturdier vampire asked, "What is agreed?"

"My love, this is Henry Gull. He has agreed to fight zombies with us."

"Ulric Barda," the vampire corrected her.

Not giving Henry the satisfaction of using the false name, she said, "Henry, this is Doctor Joseph Dante."

Joseph, aware of Avianna's coolness, withheld the offer of a handshake, but said, "Welcome to the zombie war." After a hesitation, he asked, "How did you find us?"

"One of my 'children' knows someone who knows someone who heard that the American lover of the legendary Avianna still works as a doctor—here."

Switching the subject, Joseph asked, "Do you have your own car?"

"Yes, outside."

"Then you can follow us into the Everglades."

Henry nodded and left to pull his car behind the Bentley. Anything else he had to say or wanted to do could wait.

Chapter 3

The Reporters Reunion

In her Everglades village, Keenu Kulae O'Mallory and her family filled the tiny living room/kitchenette of their treehouse. Lighter in complexion than her ebony mother, nineteen-year-old Alexandria faced Keenu. On the loveseat nearby, Keenu's blond, blue-eyed husband, Martin, sat next to their twenty-one-year-old, Johanna. Linett's surviving twin opened her Persian blue eyes wide and pulled her long blonde hair forward to lay over her slim chest.

Keenu shouted at Alexandria: "I forbid you!"

Alexandria snapped, "You can't forbid me, Mama. I'm an adult."

Wiping her hands on her apron to keep her floral dress dry, Keenu insisted, "I can and I am."

"Or what? You'll ban me from home? Well, this treehouse isn't home. Our home is hundreds of miles away and overrun with zombies. All my childhood friends—except Missy—are hiding, dead, or changed. I'm sorry if it scares you, but Missy and I have important work to do!"

As she continued washing dishes, Keenu wondered how far she should go to protect her daughter. The skin around her eyes tightened. Her throat constricted, but she choked out, "Don't let us lose another daughter, the way we lost Linett. Don't make Johanna our only child."

Johanna interrupted with, "Don't use me, Mama. Play fair."

"I'm not playing! When Alexandria and Missy went to Dohiyi to report on that battle, she lied to us about where she was! Your sister lied to us, and Missy lied to her parents." Keenu huffed at Alexandria, "Do you know how terrified we all were to learn that the two of you hiked from Williamsburg to the Blue Ridge Mountains, through zombie infested regions? And to what? To surround yourselves with supernaturals, zombies, Marines, gunfire, and napalm bombs! And why? To cover a war you're not qualified to cover! Alexandria, you and Missy are college bloggers—not Woodward or Bernstein!"

"First of all, we didn't know the supernaturals existed until much later! Second, most newspaper reporters are already lost to zombies, so the papers just regurgitate the blogs—our blogs, Mama! Whoever Woodward and Bernstein are, we're the ones that were there." She strode over to her father and pleaded, "Papa, say something."

Since Linett's death, Martin O'Mallory's normally rosy complexion had faded. His blue eyes had saddened, and his once-solid build sagged. "What do you want me to say?" he asked, "that you're lying to us about covering the battle in Dohiyi was inexcusable? Or that—," he interrupted himself to say, "I'm sorry," to Keenu. Then, he continued, "Or that I'm very proud of you."

One of the most powerful witches in the country protested, "Martin!"

He walked over and faced his wife as he explained, "I read and continue to read the girls' blogs. I see the way the mainstream press copies them. No other reporters covered the Dohiyi battle. It was pivotal, but our girls were the only ones there. Alexandria's photos and Missy's reporting gave people hope that we might survive this nightmare. They continue giving people hope with every article they post."

He reached for Keenu's hand, and she pulled it away. He moaned, "Since we lost Linett, I haven't been able to sleep. I have trouble putting two thoughts together. I walk around holding my breath; but Alexandria and Missy have the courage I've lost."

Keenu frowned at her husband. Static electricity lifted the hair on everyone's necks, wind rattled the dishes on the shelves, and sweet tea splashed out of their glasses. Outside, the black cat, Merlin, leapt from the railing into a tree.

"Keenu," Martin whispered.

The witch shuddered and closed her eyes. Everything around them quieted. She rushed out of the treehouse.

Still inside, Linett's surviving twin, Johanna, knotted her hair behind her neck. She faced her younger sister, and said, "I need you to use all the powers you know you have, and …Hell… use the ones you don't know you have, too." She hesitated then added, "Just don't make me the last sister."

"This time, we won't be alone. The president decided we should travel with Captain Nicci's units. Missy is talking to our liaison about our keeping control over our stories."

Johanna murmured, "I don't understand the president or military agreeing to this."

"Our unauthorized reports were good for the military; but, with private citizens posting photos and speculation, protecting the werewolf and vampire identities is getting tougher."

Martin interrupted, "I'm just glad you're not lying to your mama and me anymore."

"Papa, I promise to find a way to let you know we're safe; but, right now, I have to pack." In her room she began putting the few items that would fit into her flowered tote—the same one she used in Dohiyi. Before putting on the matching dress she had mended, she pulled, tugged, and yanked tights over her heavy thighs and rounded stomach.

Outside, she climbed down the ladder to the waiting transport. Knowing the men below could peek up her dress made her skin crawl, but she calmed her nerves by focusing on an egret nesting nearby. At the bottom of the ladder, she stepped into a wide, shallow boat.

She glanced up to a walkway where her mother and the wizard, Hilanor, stood. As the witch and wizard stared down at Alexandria, Keenu glared and Hilanor leaned on his black staff. Avianna had given the wizard a limb from an African Blackwood tree and he had carved it into that staff and infused it with magic.

After a quick wave at the two of them, Alexandria turned to the small boat's captain. Frowning, she protested: "I hired canoes, because I didn't want motors to impact the environment—or the noise to attract zombies."

The captain, a scrawny, old man named Gabriel, had a full head of hair. He smiled at her and said, "Don't worry 'bout this boat. There's plenty of badder stuff out here to worry 'bout."

A movement in the channel caught his eye, and he called to his two, armed guards, "Gator in that saw grass." With its belly swelled from a recent meal, they all watched it turn away.

Gabriel admonished Alexandria saying, "Poisonous snakes, scared-witless refugees, walkin'-bitin' zombies, and hungry alligators—it's crazy dainjus out here. So, a little gasoline in the water an' a little noise are not my biggest worries. Hell! If an airboat would have fit though this part of the 'glades, I would've used one!"

Without another word, Alexandria sat. Opening her tote bag, she checked the cell phones she and Missy had collected on their travels. Realizing she had left the last charged one with her mother, she groaned.

Gabriel steered the craft through narrow sloughs canopied with growth. Once the captain had steered the boat away from the protections of the treehouse village, swarming insects bit them through their insect repellent.

Longset, the heavier guard, carried a twenty-two magnum. He ducked under a six-foot long yellow snake that dangled from a low branch.

As Alexandria doubled over to protect her face, Longset pointed to the deep brown stripes and yellow eyes, saying, "Rat snake." In response, the snake hissed with a black, forked tongue.

The second guard, a bald man named Caleb, grumbled, "You going to find your way out of here, Gabriel?"

The captain grunted, "I don't know how I found my way in here, so I s'pose I won't be knowing how I'm finding my way out." He pointed at Alexandria and said, "You promised me that a friend would help me navigate. I ain't seen no friend, but I've known where to go at every turn." Agitated, he yelled above the motor, "Bite my ass if I'm not freaked 'bout all this."

Caleb growled, "An' deep 'nough water just stays with the boat. Now, Girly, you come from that witchin' place, so I'm askin' if you're a witch, and if you been doin' this?"

Alexandria squirmed under the weight of the secret that Hilanor was directing the captain's mind. Frustrated that she did not have enough power to help herself, Alexandria snapped at the captain: "Do you see a broomstick with me?"

To distract herself, Alexandria pulled out her camera. She photographed the salt-loving mangrove trees that had adapted to the brackish water in parts of the 'glades. She photographed vultures perched on their branches and an alligator drifting between beds of sawgrass. Pointing at the 'gator, she groaned, "It's huge."

Gabriel nodded and said, "'Tween zombies wanderin' into the 'glades, an' refugees rollin' off the chickees in their sleep, these critters just keep on growin'—and so do their appetites."

"Chickees?"

"Platforms on stilts. You'll see 'em, soon. The Seminoles built 'em first, but decades of storms took most of those down. Then hunters built 'em for restin' at night, and homeowners built 'em for fishin'."

Longset added, "Now they're refugee camps."

As soon as he spoke, their boat emerged from the narrow slough into a wider stretch. There, a chickee stood four feet above the shallow water with canoes tied to its supporting pillars. Among the canoes, seven alligators nudged and bit each other. A fair-skinned girl, maybe eight years old, sat on the edge of the platform with her legs tucked under her. Her long red hair needed washing, and her green dress needed mending. With a shy smile, she waved at Alexandria who took her photo and waved back.

With the boat headed into another bend, the witch's daughter shivered and perspiration beaded on her forehead. An image flashed through her mind and she shouted back at the people on the Chickee, "Get in your boats! Get off that chickee!"

Caleb growled, "Why you yelling, Girly? Even if they can hear you, they won't listen. They're desperate to get away from the zombies and 'gators. They're desperate enough to pile wives, kids, aunts, uncles, cousins onto those little platforms!"

Gabriel took their boat around the next curve without anything happening. Dread chilled Alexandria. As it intensified, she closed her eyes and hunched over her knees.

Not long after, the sound of cracking lumber filled the early evening air. Then came violent splashing, and shattering screams.

"Go back!" Alexandria yelled to the captain.

"No, Ma'am. That would be suicide."

"Go on back, now!" the young woman demanded, "There are children on that chickee. We can't leave them."

Caleb's shoulders sagged as he said, "You saw them 'gators. The second those people hit the water they were lost."

Longset grumbled, "We know what we're talking about, Child."

Alexandria's stomach churned. Her head pounded. Her chest heaved. Her throat constricted. Nearing hysteria she cried, "I can still hear them screaming. Y'all hear them, too! Please, go back!"

The boat continued to pull away from the diminishing sounds. Gabriel said, "You know how scared people be. Them parents wouldn't see that my boat's too small. They would've piled in and toppled us to the 'gators."

A vision of the green dress in bloody water shook Alexandria. Accepting that the child and her family were past saving released a steady flow of tears. Gaining control, but remaining silent, she studied marks inside the boat's bottom and inhaled the pong of wet boots and dead fish.

The familiar buzz of flies pulled her upright and she called out, "Zombies!"

'Where?"

She pointed ahead to a bend in their path, and said, "There."

Caleb protested, "Don't see any."

"Girl's right," Gabriel grunted, "I'm hearin' their flies."

The witch's daughter hugged herself.

Seconds later, a head and shoulders rose from the water alongside the boat and rotting hands reached for her.

Gabriel screamed at her, "Get down!" and the guards opened fire.

On the floor, fish oil, gasoline droplets, and spilled beer-soaked Alexandria's long curls and dress.

Diseased ones plodded through the six-inch deep marsh and crowded the boat from both sides, Gabriel set his rifle down and shifted the boat into reverse. Having distance, he stopped his craft, grabbed his rifle, and shot at every head in his line of fire.

Being in the bottom of the boat reminded Alexandria of the night she and Missy hid in a rickety shed surrounded by vultures and snarling rotters. Remembering that ghoulish night of putrid smells and dreadful sounds gagged her, but sitting in Gabriel's open boat terrified her more. She grabbed the oar near her feet and spun around, swinging at an old woman who rose from the water and grabbed for her. As she knocked the rotter backward, the captain's bullet tore away part of its skull, splattering Alexandria.

Gabriel set down his rifle to shift the boat into gear. He drove his craft forward between biters. The boat's forward thrust slammed Alexandria to the boat's bottom and dropped her into oblivion.

Uncounted hours later, her head pounding, she flinched at the sound of a heart monitor beeping and gagged on the antiseptic air. A familiar and safe whisper floated through the pitch. Alexandria opened her eyes to a blurry room. A doctor, someone she recognized from Dohiyi came into focus, with Missy at his side. Alexandria pushed sounds through her dry throat.

Missy teased, "Wow! You and I are supposed to be the ones who run away? Now, I hear you killed a zombie."

"I couldn't run on water."

"I hope you took enough pictures to make it worth the concussion."

Alexandria wanted to tell Missy that she had visualized the chickee tragedy well before the structure collapsed. Her friend would understand the significance of that. Before she could speak, another face appeared: Captain Nicci's.

"Hello, Ms. O'Mallory. Nice to see you're still alive."

Alexandria nodded and slipped back into darkness.

Chapter 4

Cross Currents

It took another week to finish the construction on the Marine's temporary base. By that time, a helicopter had brought in the werewolves. The vampires had slipped in during the night, and the witch, Keenu, and a friend had come by canoe.

With Captain James Nicci still in camp, Lieutenant Ritt called a meeting. The squad's Sergeants stood along the tent wall with John Ritt. Supernatural leaders sat at the table. The curvaceous little witch, Keenu wore a black formal. The willowy vampire, Avianna, wore a gown from 1600s. The werewolf, Mary, wearing jeans and a T-shirt snapped at the other two women, "Is overkill the new dress code?"

Keenu blushed, but Avianna smiled and said, "*Ma no.* I am never overdressed."

Tall and wiry, the thirty-seven-year-old Captain ran a hand through his graying brown hair. The number of battles he had orchestrated since Dohiyi had darkened the circles under his amber eyes. His olive complexion had paled, and he had thinned. He waited for a break in the pandemonium along the T-wall before saying, "Avianna, thank you for coming back to us. Keenu, I'm glad to finally meet you."

The vampire and witch nodded without saying anything.

The Captain continued, "Operation Clean Sweep is working. The cost in human lives has been high but would've been higher without the supernaturals fighting and sacrificing alongside us." He opened a map on the center of the table, and continued, "The Everglades has over two thousand square miles of pineland, marsh, and swamp. Other units are clearing other parts of it." He brushed his hand over a section and said, "You are tasked with clearing zombies out of this arc."

He stood straighter, made eye contact with each supernatural, and said, "You need to know that the two college reporters who released Dohiyi battle photos are here at the behest of the president."

Chairs scraped backward as all the supernaturals stood.

The Sergeants along the tent wall reached for their weapons.

Nicci raised his hands and ordered them, "At ease!" To the supernaturals, he said, "Please. Hear me out."

They sat.

He continued with, "After each battle we fought, photos or eyewitness accounts were leaked. The world already suspects that supernatural's are real. The president believes that denying it is worse than letting the reporters tell the story. After this meeting, I'm taking Keenu, Avianna, and Kristian to meet the reporters."

Keenu stared at her clasped hands.

When Avianna's brows furrowed and blue veins bulged under her translucent skin. Joseph placed his hand on the hand of the woman he loved. The vibrant green in her eyes softened and her skin reverted to human paleness.

Nicci hid his relief under the stern warning, "This coalition has to hold together: no excuses and no choice."

Avianna's Neapolitan accent thickened as she purred, "Captain, you know that the wolves do not walk on water. You know we vampires do not tolerate the sun. Yet here we are in the Everglades. It feels like *un test di lealtà.*"

Joseph translated: "A test of loyalty."

Nicci forced himself to stare into the eyes that aroused most men, himself included. He steadied himself to say, "Avianna, this is not a test. We need your speed, agility, and survivability to help us exterminate the zombies here. You'll go out with Sergeant Kowolski's and Sergeant Prem Kunchai's squads. I've had hooded jump-suits and gloves made to protect your people from the sun. I've also requisitioned boats with roofs."

Studying the werewolves and allowing Mary's golden loveliness to charm him, he explained, "I am counting on you and the other werewolves to patrol with Sergeant Max Schwinn's squad on the semisolid ground around the main bodies of water." He waited for a break in the gunfire blasts along the wall.

Addressing the witch, Nicci said, "Keenu, while the Wiccan community supports us from your village, I appreciate that you—and I'm told a wizard you know—have agreed to work here."

Avianna confronted Keenu. Her eyes brightened, and blue veins darkened under her skin. This time, Joseph did not try to restrain her. Tensing for a fight, the werewolves scraped their chairs back from the table. Nicci's Sergeants reached for their sidearms. Ignoring them, the vampire leader hissed at the witch, "You brought Hilanor?"

The witch stood as well. Her shoulder-length curls floated in an unnatural breeze. Her eyes sparkled as she said, "He insisted on coming."

Avianna snarled, "He is over a hundred years old, and you are putting him in a boat surrounded by alligators to fight zombies. *Incoscienza incredibile!*"

Nicci shouted, "Whatever you're saying—."

Joseph added, "Inconceivable recklessness."

Nicci bellowed, "Stop! Stop the insults and the arguing. We're here to kill zombies—not each other. Both of you stay. Lieutenant Ritt, stay. Kristian and Joseph, please wait outside. The rest of you are dismissed. We start in two days with a 0600 meeting."

After everyone else filed out, the Captain demanded of the women, "Explain! Without the wind, heavy accent, blue veins, and all that shit!"

As the wind dissipated, the vampire's skin regained opacity.

Keenu clarified, "Hilanor and Avianna have a romantic history. While she's still very protective, he doesn't want to stay in the background the way he did in Dohiyi."

"Avianna, you have history with this wizard?" the Captain asked.

Reverting to sensual playfulness, the vampire simmered, "*Sì,* in his youth: *gil amanti:* lovers. I will leave the details to your imagination. We are now *amici:* friends."

Nicci's body responded. He needed a breath to regain control.

The silent witch withheld from the Captain that Hilanor, in Dohiyi, had blocked her from knowing her daughters were there—the daughter who fought the zombies, and the one who photographed the battle from a nearby building. That deception had cut the witch like a blade.

The vampire continued, "Joseph knows about Hilanor, but reminding him would be *maldestro*, no? What is it the French say? Gauche?"

'Great,' the Captain thought, 'a love-triangle with the most powerful creatures in his war.' Just before Keenu averted her eyes, a flicker in them told Nicci that she hid something. "All right," Nicci concluded, "Avianna, Keenu, please come with me. Kristian will represent the werewolves and come with us to see the reporters."

Kristian, who had waited at a junction in the walkways, joined them.

The reporters' room occupied a corner in the closest building to the T-wall. The Captain regretted not finding a quieter place for them. Nicci called, "Ladies, are you ready for us?"

Missy's voice called back, "Sure."

Nicci and Ritt entered first.

In the room, the girls sat on a twin bed. Alexandria's camera and Missy's notes lay on the other bed. Blonde, blue-eyed Missy wore jeans, a denim shirt, and cowboy boots. Alexandria, with a complexion like dark honey, wore tan angle boots and a floral sundress trimmed in embroidered pink roses against an ivory background.

Kristian entered next. Over six feet tall, he was broad only in the shoulders. His trim mustache and beard accented a square jaw and full lips. His shoulder-length platinum hair glowed in the dim lighting, and his steel-blue eyes scanned the room.

The girls' eyes stayed on him.

The vampire entered next.

Then the witch.

Nicci started to speak but Alexandria breathed a strangled, "Mama."

Missy murmured, "Hello, Miss Keenu."

Nicci sputtered, "Mama? Miss Keenu—what the fuck is going on here? Why the hell didn't I know about this?"

Keenu explained, "I'm Keenu Kulae …O'Mallory, Alexandria's mother. I had ordered my daughter to stay out of battle zones and did not suspect she was here until you mentioned college reporters." Another wind shifted objects in the room, toppling over and rolling a mug that crashed to the floor.

"Mama! Please calm down!"

In a hardened voice, Keenu responded, "You do not belong in another battle, young lady. Especially not here, where there are too many ways to die!"

Alexandria challenged her mother: "If you'd let me into your coven, I might be stronger by now."

"With your second sight so limited, you're not ready to join the coven."

"The others are Wiccan, not witches, so what's the difference?"

"They add their strength to mine and stabilize me! You, child, bang on my nerves!"

Nicci yelled, "Enough! Sit! Now!" Focusing on Alexandria, he asked, "How much do you know about your mother's role in all this?" He raised a hand to slender, blonde Missy, and to Keenu, to quell any interruptions. Objects in the room settled.

Alexandria blurted out, "My mama's a witch. She's a coven leader and member of--." Her mother's glare stopped her.

"And the others?"

Alexandria shook her head, "I don't know them." She tried to say more but lost balance.

Missy reached out a hand to steady her friend.

With narrowed eyes and furrowed brows, the witch's daughter scrutinized Kristian and Avianna.

Missy murmured, "Alex, what do you see?"

Alexandria pointed at Kristian, saying, "He's the wolf we photographed at Dohiyi. But not a wolf: a werewolf!" She pointed at Avianna and hissed, "From where we hid, we couldn't see under the trees in the amphitheater, but that's where she and others like her fought. Missy, she's a vampire! I can see what she is and the horrible way she shredded infected people."

Afraid her daughter might envision Linett's death, Keenu knelt beside her. Her hand trembled as she touched Alexandria's hair. A breeze rippled through the blankets and ruffled their clothing and hair. The coffee pot rattled on the hot plate. The girls' hairbrushes and two charging cell phones slid across the end tables. The witch pleaded, "No more, Alexandria. You must stop seeing Dohiyi, now."

Alexandria lifted her tear-streaked face toward her mother and whispered, "Too late." She stood. Dizzy and swaying, she cried, "My sister trusted you, but you didn't save her. Do you know what I'm seeing? What I'm hearing? What I'm smelling? It's Linett. It's her pleas, her blood, her torn…"

Before the girl finished, the vampire crossed the space between them, and grasped the sides of Alexandria's head. The vampire's mind froze everyone in the room. She reached into the girl's thoughts. With her accent thickened, she murmured, "Listen to my voice. You will know how your sister died without seeing her end. You will never again hear or smell her demise. You will know that, though I failed her, I loved her." Still holding Alexandria's head, she buried every vision of Linett's death. Then she intoned, "You will know the pain of your concussion, but you will not sicken." She eased the dazed young woman back into her seat. Only then did the vampire release everyone in the room.

Nicci snarled, "IF YOU EVER IMMOBILIZE ME OR MY PEOPLE, AGAIN, I will personally shish kebob your heart!"

"*Perdonami,* Captain. I am sorry for the invasion, but I required stillness to help the girl."

Alexandria's concussed head pounded, but long, deep breaths eased her nausea. Turning on Avianna, she said, "You caused my sister's death."

"*Sì.* I went to Joseph instead of Linett. I will always—" A floor-shaking volley of gunfire drowned out the rest of her admission.

Nicci glowered at one supernatural after the other then demanded, "No more secrets. Tell me, NOW, anything else I should know."

Keenu began to speak but Avianna interjected, "We have another vampire with us. He calls himself Ulric Barda."

"The Dracula imitator?"

"*Sì.* Five of us went into Dohiyi, but four came out. He makes us five again."

Keenu blurted, "Is Kahl-maus here again?"

"If he is in the area, he is not coming close enough for me to sense his presence."

Nicci addressed everyone in the room, "Whatever you feel about each other, control it. Whatever your histories are with each other, shelve them. In two days, we start a sweep of the Everglades. This mission is too important to let anything else matter. Go to your tents and let these girls rest."

He frowned at Keenu, "And that means you too. Everyone out but these young ladies!"

Kristian left without hesitation.

As Avianna left, she glanced back at Nicci with an amused smile that reminded the Captain of how little control he had over her.

Keenu followed the vampire.

The girls stayed on the bed, with Missy hugging Alexandria.

Nothing in Nicci's military career taught him to manage a supernatural soap opera. Walking out with Ritt, the Captain said, "Send someone in later to clear out the extra chairs and have the doctor check on Alexandria's concussion. Who knows what that vamp did inside her head?" Then he murmured, "All this is yours now, Lieutenant. Keep reminding them that they're here to kill the diseased ones and not each other."

Ritt grunted, "Ooh Rah."

In the front of the encampment, guards chased black vultures away from the tires of Nicci's armored command vehicle. For decades, the birds had torn at the vinyl and rubber components in Florida's vehicles and boats. A Marine shot a vulture and the others took flight. No one wanted to kill too many of nature's clean-up crew.

Nicci climbed into the CV to go to the next two camps where other officers led squads with contingents of supernaturals. Nicci's armored CV wove through a herd of rotters coming toward its vibrations. The gunner on top of the vehicle razed zombies with neither hesitation nor celebration. Ritt understood the gunner's stoicism. Although the abominations had once been teachers, physicians, builders, technicians, artists, and musicians, their eradication had become perfunctory.

In the main camp, Ritt went back into his tent to review the latest reports. Every branch of the armed forces worked around missing ranks. U.S. Marine units and U.S. Naval Reserves had spread inward from the West Coast. The Air Force and Army Reserves had worked their way north from the southern border and coastline. The Army and Air Force Reserves had advanced North from a southern staging ground. Special Forces units swept inward from the East Coast. Naval Reserves and Seals cleared rivers, lakes, and islands.

Every Coast Guard boat in service, and every fixable one from the yards, deployed to clear the beaches along U.S. coasts. In the middle of the country other specialized units covered different terrains. After the military cleared areas, the local National Guard, police, and courageous civilians held them. Ritt listened to the shots fired by the perimeter guards. Thinking about the biters coming from the nearby suburban neighborhoods, he mumbled to himself, "Endless."

Chapter 5

Smoke and Promises

Kahl-maus's previous attempts to transform children had resulted in their permanent deaths or produced mindless demolishers. He had succeeded with only two young ones. In a run-down camper hidden in the Everglades, they sat at a stained enamel table. The boy peered through a bug-crusted window and wondered if he had heard a voice outside. He had black, curly hair, and his worn clothing hung on his emaciated body. Dying of aids, he had begged Kahl-maus to turn him into a vampire. Then he allowed himself to be renamed Adam.

Across the table, the girl fidgeted with her torn T-shirt and shoved her hands into her faded jeans pockets. She had limp brown hair and dull, red-rimmed, brown eyes. Kahl-maus and Adam had found her beaten and raped. She had struggled against Kahl-maus turning her and hated being renamed Eve.

Adam stood and said, "Let's go," and Eve followed him down the narrow passage to the cramped bedroom.

There, a sixteen-year-old girl waited.

After Adam cracked open the only window.

The teen on the bed said, "You promised me immortality."

Adam explained, "All you need to do is follow instructions. Do what we told you to do and say what we told you to say."

Pouting, she said, "I thought I would be bitten."

Adam lied: "This is a different way."

The girl knelt on the bed. Her dry, bleached hair hung to her shoulders, and her frayed cotton dress sagged against the small curves beneath it. Inflamed track marks dotted both forearms. She closed her eyes and, through cracked lips, intoned, "Kahl-maus, father and creator, come to me. Possess me. Speak through me."

Standing in the doorway, Eve rolled her eyes and Adam gave his sister a silencing glance.

A black mist appeared in the window's opening. Slowly the mist spilled down the wall and pooled on the bed. It moved along the spread to the front of the girl who waited with outstretched arms.

Following previous instructions, the girl kept her eyes closed and tilted back her head. She opened her mouth wide.

The mist floated up the front of her body and hovered above her face. After a brief hesitation, it cascaded into her mouth and nose.

She gasped. Her eyes opened wide. As the mist continued to flow into her, she squeezed her eyes shut and opened them again. She leaned sideways, and then she reached upward as though she was climbing an invisible ladder. Her face blued, but the remaining mist flowed into her.

Adam frowned, and Eve closed her eyes.

The girl spasmed and clawed at her throat. As her lungs filled, her eyes bulged and teared. She arched backward, stretched her neck, flipped her head side-to-side, and collapsed.

Like lava from Mt. Vesuvius, Kahl-maus erupted from his victim's nose and mouth. He spiraled toward the ceiling and dipped toward the bed, before flowing out the open window.

His helpless disciples froze in the doorway.

Eve stammered, "M-maybe we needed someone stronger."

"This isn't about strength. This is about a witch cursing our sire. If we keep trying to help him, the witch might come after us, next. For now, let's clean this up."

They carried the body outside and rolled it into a rivulet for the nearest alligators to find.

The blackened mist drifted toward them. Using the telepathy of their sire-bond, Kahl-maus said, "We will postpone any more attempts at possession, and you will help me have my vengeance."

"How?" Eve asked.

"I will tell you when the time comes."

***

Hours later, Adam and Eve sat at their rickety table. Their extreme need for blood had shriveled their skin and yellowed their eyes.

Eve frowned and said, "We should have taken a soldier."

"I'm hungry, too, but Father doesn't want us to let the Marines know we're here—not yet."

The girl protested, "He was younger than us when he was turned. He's certainly not my father."

"You're only brave enough to say that because he left. Eve, this is all he's asked us to do."

"Pimping girls for him to suffocate, and sacrificing babies—you call that all? Well, he's going to want more from us. You know it. I want to be able to say 'no' like Avianna can."

"Other vamps have told us that Avianna's an aberration. Sires should have control of their children, but Avianna's sire bond never formed. She has defied Father for over eight-hundred years, but we already know we can't. Eve . . . we can't. That's the end of it."

Eve frowned out the window, hating the truth.

Chapter 6

Jamaica's Quest

After receiving permission from his alphas, Jamaica Savann left the werewolf community and drove for hours. With his GPS losing the signal, he relied on a map and his wolf instincts.

The first guarded neighborhood had Victorian-style homes in pastel colors. Scattered window boxes had vegetables growing. Every house had a rain catcher made from barrels or coolers. Lights in the windows indicated that they had power.

In the next neighborhood, charred buildings rose from sidewalks littered with glass shards and stained with blood. The stench of death fouled the air. Abominations lumbered off the sidewalks toward the sound of his car. Jamaica pressed the gas pedal and darted around the pack.

A mile later, he found a well-maintained street where eight armed civilians lined the sidewalks on each side of the road. They all pointed their weapons in his direction. Jamaica caught his breath and stiffened. Strong postures and correctly extended guns identified the experienced ones. Full extensions with high-compression postures betrayed the amateurs. The werewolf kept the car rolling forward. As he pulled alongside them, they opened fire. He ducked.

The bullets did not hit his car, but he turned in his seat to see a dozen zombies dropping behind him. A plow with a bucket grapple, and a dump truck, came from a side street and scooped the bodies from the street.

The werewolf wiped perspiration from his forehead and waved to the guards on the street. He called, "Thank you," but kept driving. To reach Covington, Kentucky, he needed the only train running on the right tracks.

As Jamaica rounded a corner, the vestige of a woman stumbled off the sidewalk in front of his car. He angled the car to go around her but gunfire raked the street and the woman. Bullets hit his car.

Roaring, "Shit! Shit! Shit!" he ducked along the front seat and let the car roll backwards until the gunfire stopped. Sitting up, he stared at the shredded woman who twisted on the asphalt. The werewolf rolled down his window, letting in a gust of gasoline fumes.

A balding man called from a third-floor balcony, "Sorry I hit your car."

A gray-haired woman shouted from a ground floor window, "With Annie Oakley up there saving you, you're now driving a sieve." Then she pointed to a side street, saying, "Go on down to headquarters. They'll arrange for you to take over the payments on an abandoned house and they'll find you a car and online work. We have a bank, a general store, a pharmacy, and the train station—all guarded by people who can hit what they aim at."

"Thank you, anyway, but I just need the station."

The gray head leaned further out the window to point and said, "Then go another block and turn right onto West Innes Street. Next, turn right onto Depot Street, and hurry. Your car isn't getting far. Good luck."

Jamaica waived, closed his window, and steered the car away from the woman's body.

A block from the station, the car's engine sputtered to a stop. After placing the portable GPS in his duffle bag, Jamaica searched the immediate area for zombies. Seeing none, he left the car and ran to the station entrance, where attendants opened the gate for him.

Guards inside directed him to the strip-search booth where a jittery attendant checked the imposing man for bites. Not finding any, he said, "Use your credit card to open the train door."

Even before the zombie infection spread, members of Jamaica's pack had liquidated their assets to create a reserve that paid for the land, cabin construction, food, and travel expenses. When the married alphas, Mary and Kristian, sanctioned Jamaica's trip, they gave him a credit card.

Jamaica looked around, and then boarded. Able to smell a hundred times better than humans, and sensitive to individual pheromone scents, he could identify prey almost two miles away. Werewolf hearing helped him distinguish animal and human sounds six to ten miles away. With the thirteen passengers inside the train smelling healthy, he swiped the credit card to open the door. He settled into a booth and dropped his duffle bag on the floor between his feet.

According to bloggers, people who fled Cincinnati often ended up in Covington, on the Kentucky side of the Ohio river. The city had established a refugee camp and offered them abandoned homes and jobs. An orphanage in the camp housed the children who came without family. If Jamaica's wife and son had stayed alive long enough to flee Cincinnati, Jamaica needed to search for them in Covington.

The werewolf's eyes closed, and memories of the battle to save Dohiyi filled his dreams. As a four-hundred-pound wolf, he ran down alleys crowded with rotters. Broken glass nicked his foot pads. Saliva dripped from between his sharp teeth, and his long tongue hung out—cooling him.

Then he stood, in human form, in a dark space where women sat within a ring of flickering pillar candles. The witch and Wiccans recited incantations that energized him, but also instilled dread. The smell and snarls of zombies filled the void behind him.

Jamaica jolted awake.

The engine had slowed. Groaning metal, human howls, and the stench told the werewolf that the zombie-mover—a modified cattle-catcher on the front of every train—had pushed rotters to the sides of the track.

When a swarm of flies hit the windows, passengers took the nearest children to the floor. The scent of fear permeated the car and enflamed the wolf within Jamaica. To hide the gold in his eyes, he lowered himself and ducked his head.

Every child had been taught that noise brought death. Four rows behind Jamaica, a man whispered to a young boy, "Let's play the quiet game. If you can stay down and quiet longer than me, you will win a candy." Ducking below the window level, the adult did not see the number of creatures that emerged from the woods.

The engineers eased the train forward, until the herd fell behind. As the train increased speed, passengers found their seats. Adults comforted themselves by hugging the children with them. Jamaica imagined his wife and child alive and in his arms.

Without realizing he had fallen asleep again, the train's lurching to a stop woke him.

Outside the window, armed guards circled the station platform.

As the werewolf left the train, the wind shifted and carried the stench from burning bodies a quarter mile away. Jamaica stepped into yet another line for another strip search.

Enough passengers dispersed from the station that the next train used only one car. Jamaica took the empty bench seat facing a young woman and a girl about five years old. The werewolf detected the pheromones that linked the woman and child. Thinking of the wife and son he abandoned, he shuddered and closed his eyes.

Breathing hard, the woman shrank into her seat.

Wanting to ease her fear, Jamaica opened his eyes and flashed a quick smile. Softening his voice, he said, "Don't be afraid. I just want to find my family in Covington."

While the little girl kept her face buried in her mother's yellow skirt, the woman offered the shaky explanation: "My husband is…gone," she said, "and I received a message from my brother to join them." When Jamaica nodded, she continued, "He and his family made it to my parents' house, but I'm not sure why I'm telling you this; it's awfully private for casual conversation."

Jamaica said, "People need connection." He had to push himself to add, "I don't know if my wife or son are still alive." Withholding that he had abandoned them, he said, "We had already separated before the infection began."

"I'm sorry. How old is your boy?"

"He's eleven, if he's…." He did not finish.

"I know. I know. The pandemic has made us all a little crazy. Like, I keep wondering why we call them zombies. Don't zombies come out of graves? These things are just sick people who don't die all the way." Her eyes teared, and she stopped talking.

Jamaica nodded and let her stay quiet.

The little girl climbed onto her mother's lap, crumpling the young woman's skirt. It exposed her mother's slim thigh, and the woman struggled to adjust her clothing and shift the child into a more comfortable position.

Jamaica faced the window and wondered what he should say if he found his family alive. Would they believe that, after a werewolf bit him, he fled the city to keep from hurting them? Even if they believed him, would they forgive him for staying away when Cincinnati became infected? His racing pulse would bring out the gold in his eyes, so he closed them.

The train reached its next stop. Jamaica sniffed the air before disembarking. An armed guard stood near-by, and Jamaica asked him about Covington.

"You're an hour and a half away by bus."

Jamaica waited in one body-search line, while the young mother gave Jamaica a trembling smile from another queue. A flash of himself as a zombied werewolf attacking the little girl soaked him in dread.

When the security guard finished searching Jamaica for bites, the man assured him, "You're fine, sir. You can board the bus, now."

As soon as Jamaica took a seat, the woman from the train took the seat next to him and sat her daughter on her lap. She smiled and said, "Hello, again."

Believing the young mother would not trust him if she knew what he was, he kept his "Hello" quiet and uninviting.

Two armed guards climbed to the roof and buckled their security straps around the railings. The bus eased forward. In the air-conditioning, the little girl hugged her mom and fell asleep. The young woman, in a somber voice, said: "She never cries anymore, never asks for anything. All she wants is sleep. I have to bully her to eat."

For the first time, Jamaica noticed the warmth in the woman's brown eyes and the way her dark waves of thick hair framed her lovely face. Turning his attention back to the child, he said, "We'd all like to sleep until the zombies are gone."

She nodded.

Turning his face away, he snapped at the woman, "Get down."

Breathing hard, she pulled her daughter to the floor. The little girl did not protest.

Other people in the car shouted, "What's going on?"

Someone closer to the front shouted, "Out the window! Oh my God!"

As the driver shifted into reverse and rolled the bus backward, someone yelled, "Don't back up! Don't back up! They're behind us, too!"

Jamaica hissed, "Keep quiet. No crying, no screaming, no yelling. Everyone out of sight."

Adults pulled children to the floor as five people brought out guns. The ones who were armed crouched below the windows without dropping to the floor. The bus driver cut her engine and ducked. Zombies shuffled abreast then passed the silent bus. The passengers' fears triggered adrenalin surges in the werewolf.

With the moon almost full, his rapid heart-beat and surging blood changed the gold flecks in his eyes to solid yellow and made the hair on the back of his hands grow. His lips pulled back from still-human teeth. He ducked and trembled with the effort to stop the change.

Just then, a tiny hand touched his leg. The child, looking like a little princess in her pretty pink dress, whispered, "Don't be afraid. I won't make noise."

His eyes returned to hazel and he lost himself in the little girl's gaze. Her concern became cool water on his fires. When his hands returned to human, he whispered, "Thank you."

A baby wailed, and the abominations pivoted toward the sound.

Passengers gasped as the zombies clawed at the sides of the bus, rocking it. The people with guns rolled down the windows to shoot, letting flies swarm inside. Unarmed passengers covered any child near them.

On the roof, the guards shattered their silence with a round of gunfire. Bodies piled in the bus's path. Jamaica hurried to the driver, shouting, "Can you go over or around them?"

The middle-aged driver, with snow-white hair, shouted, "I'm not supposed to drive over them because they might snag under us."

"This is a new bus with good clearance. Try, before there are more zombies on the ground."

The driver shifted into first gear and inched the bus forward. Forcing the clawing creatures to the sides, she eased the bus over the lowest pile.

Jamaica leaned on the console, "Can you tell the guards on the roof to stop piling up bodies in front of us!"

She grabbed the mic, "Terrance, Jake, stop shooting ahead. I have to get through."

The few armed passengers fired out the open windows at the rotters who rocked both sides of the bus. Each time the bus bumped over a body, passengers gasped. Someone in the back moaned, "We're going to get stuck. Oh, Lord! We're going to get stuck."

The passengers' whimpers pumped another wave of adrenaline through the werewolf.

Afraid to look back and let them see the gold in his eyes, Jamaica snarled over his shoulder, "Knock it off! We're fine." Worried about what the driver might see, he angled his face away from her. He grabbed a rag from under the dashboard and swatted at the flies on the inside of the windshield, trying not to smear them against the glass.

With fewer biters ahead of her, the driver hit the gas pedal, propelling the bus away from the zombie mob. The flies left the bus to stay with easier meals. Shooters put their guns away. Everyone rose from the floor and collapsed in their seats with audible sighs.

Controlling his pulse stopped the change. Jamaica sat on the seat next to the mother and child. Nestled against her mom, the little girl reached out and rested a soft hand on Jamaica's arm. The child and the werewolf slept until the bus pulled into Covington station. There, the ten-foot cement walls, and armed guards should have made the passengers feel protected; it did not. Jamaica smelled their fear.

He disembarked and scowled at the rising gibbous moon. When it was full, he would have to change. A tug on his sleeve made him look down.

The little girl smiled and said, "Goodbye, Mister. I hope you find your son."

Her mother reached with trembling hand and grasped his. Then she whispered, "You have no idea what this means. She's only spoken twice since we saw her father attacked. Both times she spoke, it was to you."

"Stay safe," he said, knowing the absurdity of the sentiment.

Someone called and the woman and child turned to wave at the driver of a car. He waved back and they ran to him. Soon the car and the child who had captured his heart pulled away and left the lot. He would never know her fate and wondered if that was for the best.

Jamaica shook his head and approached a frowning man with a gray beard. The werewolf asked, "If my family reached Covington, where should I look for them?"

Lifting his patrolman's hat to push escaping gray hair back under the band, he answered, "If your wife and son came together, they'd go to the refugee camp in Devou Park. If your son came alone, there's an orphanage there."

"How far?"

Tapping the map on the station wall, he answered, "About ten miles west, but you should hide here for the night. There are zombies in the abandoned buildings down that street. Don't go in them. Just use a fire escape to reach the roof." He assessed Jamaica's tall frame and broad shoulders. Then, he added, "I'd bet on you to make it."

With his duffle bag in hand, Jamaica headed toward the abandoned buildings. His hearing and sense of smell told him that bodies rotted in every direction. Two blocks from the station, the buzz of flies and proximity to decay assaulted his senses. He jumped to the nearest fire escape ladder and climbed. Below him, five biters staggered into view.

Before he reached the third-floor landing, a rifle poked out the window. "Go back, now," a woman shouted, "or I'll shoot."

Jamaica assessed the barrel angle. With his wolf-blood pumping, he leapt the remaining steps and grabbed the weapon. He yanked the rifle from her grip and it went off. The bullet went wild. As the woman backed out of sight, he grumbled, "I'm just going to the roof to escape biters. I'll return your damn rifle on my way back down."

"We're freakin' dead if you don't!"

Another voice called out, "Mister, please. We need the rifle to keep out the rotters—and to keep the gangs away from my sister."

The mother scolded her son for saying too much.

"I'll tell you what," Jamaica said, "I only need a place to sleep. I'll keep the rifle out here. Tomorrow, I'll give your weapon back to you before leaving to search for my family. Okay?"

After a long silence, the woman murmured, "Okay."

She reached through the clean curtains to shut the window. Her graceful hands fumbled with the latch. Outside her window, Jamaica slumped into a sitting position against the wall, with the rifle across his legs. He pulled the duffle bag close to take out a pear. Below him a large group of the almost-dead shuffled past. After they left, he detected a different group: ten unwashed humans.

One twenty-something yelled, "Yo! What's up there? Up there, third floor landing. Your ol' lady kick you out?"

Another one yelled, "Maybe you gotta pay us a fine just for breathing our air."

A third said, "He ain't kicked out. He's guardin'."

A fourth yelled, "What you guardin'?"

This time, Jamaica did not stop his faster pulse from infusing gold into his eyes. Staring over the railing, he snarled, "Keep walking."

The first one yelled, "Yeah? You think you can take us all, Bro?"

Another one whispered, "Something's weird about his eyes? They ain't right."

Jamaica fired. His bullet chipped the sidewalk in the center of them, and he yelled, "I missed on purpose. Fire back and you're dead."

They scattered, with the smallest of them pulling a gun. One of his buddies hissed, "Rigs, don't shoot! No more shooting!"

As the young man took aim, Jamaica shot him in the arm. Under his screams, the werewolf heard flies.

Jamaica snarled, "You boys better run."

The one who had guessed Jamaica was guarding something yelled, "Rigs, quit screaming, or I'll fucking shoot you myself." Even without enough flies to predict zombies, he called to the others, "We've made a racket. We have to go. Go! Go! Go! Now!"

They bolted in the same direction as rotters who had come through the alley earlier. Ten minutes later the night filled with gunfire and screams.

Jamaica hunkered down to rest.

The window opened.

Jamaica pretended to be asleep as the woman covered him with a blanket. Without a word, she re-latched the window.

At sunrise, he wrapped the rifle in the woman's blanket and left to continue traveling west.

The station guard had said the refugee camp was ten miles away. Someone on the train had said that the army was plowing north from Kentucky's southern border and were still a week away from Covington. In a zombie-infested world, a ten-mile walk could become a death march.

He ran four more blocks before the buzz of flies sent another rush of adrenaline through him. He climbed the nearest fire escape ladder. He did not stop climbing until he reached the roof. From there, he found an unobstructed view of a park. Leaping rooftops, he reached the building closest to the park. After climbing down a fire escape, he sprinted toward the park and did not stop until he arrived at a tall gate with armed guards. Raising his hands, he called out, "I'm not bitten. I'm just trying to find Siloah and Jaylan Savann." The guards stared at him, so he offered: "Wait a half hour: then test me. When I'm still lucid, you'll know I wasn't bitten."

They nodded, kept their guns on him, and waited.

Jamaica caught a scent. He yelled to the guards, "Something's coming!"

A tall, husky boy ambled into view. He wore his college football jersey and carried his helmet in his hand. The vacant-eyed boy had a bite on his cheek and blood pouring down the front of his uniform.

Flies came with the football player, and one vulture circled above.

As the young rotter approached, Jamaica thought about his son and cringed.

Gun shots exploded from behind the werewolf. Together the guards put at least eight bullets into the innocent boy. The wolf changed his stare from the rotter to the guards. In Dohiyi, Captain Nicci's sharpshooters would have used one bullet; they would not have wasted ammunition or desecrated the body.

The vulture landed and began feeding. It's indestructible digestive system would process the diseased meal into acidic waste. The acid would cleanse bacteria wherever the bird left its waste.

The other guard yelled to Jamaica, "You still healthy?"

"Yes, and I still need to find my wife and son."

The gate opened and Jamaica walked through. He glanced back to see the guards dragging the corpse away from the vulture. To control infection and keep humans from being treated like food, most communities had a place to burn the bodies.

A short walk brought the werewolf into a garden paradise where tulips lined the walkways. Lilies surrounded the pond and hyacinths lined the fencing. Parents picnicked on the grass with their youngsters. Other children romped on a playground.

Across the park, a sign read, 'Registration Building.'

Jamaica thought about his wife and son not being there and the camp becoming a dead end. He resisted the urge to lie down on the sweet grass and not find out. Instead, he kept walking.

Inside the building, a short woman with curly, gray hair, wearing a candy-striped summer dress, asked, "Yes? Whom do you want? The names?"

"Savann," he murmured, "Siloah Savann." He refrained from adding 'my wife,' because Jamaica Savann had disappeared from his bloodied cab years before and might be listed as dead.

The clerk opened a ledger, asking, "Did she come from Cincinnati or somewhere else?"

"From Cincinnati, with a child—a boy."

"Do you have an approximate date?"

"No."

Without pressing him, she bent to the task of scanning through entries. She flipped page after page, running twisted fingers down each list. She kept turning pages. When she had turned more than she had left, one of Jamaica's tears fell on the corner of a page. The clerk dabbed the water spot with a tissue and kept scanning. Meeting his eyes, she said, "I'm so sorry. No Siloah Savann. Check with friends and family or go over to the orphanage."

She shrugged her shoulders, adding, "Before they closed the city, the police, National Guard, neighbors, even the gangs brought orphans out. The orphanage is diagonally across the lawn. Bending down, she brought up a sealed, plastic water bottle. "Please drink this. You look dehydrated."

Jamaica took the water with a grateful smile. On the stairs outside, indecision gripped him. What if his wife was alive somewhere else or zombied? After drinking the water, he discarded the empty bottle into the recycling bin. He paused to inhale the floral scents around him. The refugees had recreated civilization.

Praying that his wife had hung onto life—somewhere--he took a deep breath and crossed the lawn toward the orphanage.

Chapter 7

Jaylan Savann

The close-shaven, heavyset young clerk swiveled toward his computer and said, "Name please. Not yours. The child you want."

"Jaylan Savann."

The clerk, his eyes flickering with changes on the screen, asked, "Your name and relationship?"

Since he was supposed to be dead, Jamaica froze.

"You can't go near the children without me documenting your identity."

Not knowing if his brother was dead, Jamaica blurted out, "Devan Savann."

After a computer search, the clerk pushed a button on the phone and said, "Devan Savann's here for Jaylan Savann."

Jamaica shuddered. Would they have given his child to any pedophile who faked a name? Perspiration beaded his skin as he wondered what to say to the eleven-year-old he had abandoned when the boy was five.

A voice came from behind him: "Who are you?"

Jamaica evaluated the stranger who shouldered Jamaica's old backpack. The lapsed dad did not recognize his boy's long, thin frame, or dreadlocks, but he recognized the large, dark eyes, he gave him and the sculptured lips inherited from his mother. The boy's coloring came somewhere between his father's charcoal and his mother's taupe. The large man faltered before saying, "I'm Devan—your father's brother."

Stepping back, Jaylan shook his head, "Mom said Dad's relatives stayed in Jamaica."

"I came looking for family."

"Where're you taking me?"

Avoiding another lie, he said, "I'm needed in Florida."

The clerk interrupted with, "Is he family, Jaylan?"

"He looks like Mom's picture of Dad, so maybe he's my father's twin."

"Then go with him. We have ten children in rooms meant for four. We've run out of clothing and don't know when we'll run out of food. If you have anywhere else to go, go."

Jaylan scowled but followed Jamaica outside.

A volunteer stopped walking to give them water bottles. Another stopped to give them fresh apples. After gratefully accepting both, Jamaica walked to a bench and said, "Let's sit." The reddish green Liberty apples and the water cooled him. He finished his and handed his son the empty bottle, saying, "Keep the bottles in your backpack, in case we can refill them."

Jaylan put both empties into his pack, asking, "Now, what?"

"I have a promise to keep in the Everglades—Florida."

"What promise?"

"To help the military and my friends."

Jaylan glared at him and asked, "You came all the way from Jamaica Island to Cincinnati? You came to rescue me from a guarded park with food and a clean bed to take me to a swamp surrounded by zombies?"

"Sorry."

"Well, this sounds like a sucky rescue!"

"Hey, Mister, watch your language."

"M . . .m . . .my dad used to say, 'Hey, Mister.'" The boy glared at him and added, "You look like the picture—maybe too much like the picture."

Not knowing how his son would react to the truth, the werewolf said, "Twins. And I don't have time for this. Come with me or go back inside."

"You have a gun?"

"I have one."

"Then, come with me, because I need one."

"You're only eleven years old!"

"I ran with gangs and defended myself for two years. Can you tell me I'm safer unarmed?"

"No. No, I can't, but if you can buy a knife, buy one. Up close, they're better."

"Man, don't you see how short I am? Shit! I'm not knifing any adults in the head anytime soon."

Without knowing the street cost of a gun, the werewolf gave half his cash to his son.

Jaylan led Jamaica for three more blocks before telling him, "Hide." The eleven-year-old approached the side of a dented and graffiti-covered mail truck. He spoke to the driver who said something into a walkie talkie. The truck's side door opened. A man handed over a weapon and Jaylan checked the gun's weight and aim. After haggling over the prices of the weapon and ammunition, he paid. Then he loaded the revolver and returned to his father. Without hesitation, he gave back twenty-five percent of the gifted money.

Jamaica's guilt for abandoning the boy twisted into pride. Having gone to save a child, Jamaica found a survivor. After the truck left, Jamaica and Jaylan headed for the train station. When they hid from a passing herd, the boy stayed calm—even with flies on him. Father and son reached the station without wasting a shot.

After routine body checks, they boarded the bus and found a seat. Settled in, Jaylan asked, "So, it took you all this time to come for me."

"It only matters that I'm here."

"Not good enough," the boy insisted. Then, without flinching, he added, "My father was killed before the infection and Mom zombied right after the outbreak, but I survived. So, why do I need you?"

Jamaica's memories of his wife's smile, her gentle touch, and her soft kisses slammed like a fist into his chest.

"You didn't even know my mother, so why are you crying?"

"I'm tired. I'm sad. That's all."

The young voice hardened to say, "Don't lie to me!"

"Jaylan, I've lost people, too, but I'm not ready to talk about it, yet."

Jaylan squinted out his window at distant rotters attracted to the sound of the bus. "So," he said, "we take our chances together. But the unbitten one finishes the bitten one—right?"

Jamaica choked out, "Right." In the silence that followed, waves of love, guilt, and grief washed through him.

His son stared at him.

As a diversion, Jamaica asked, "You're really only eleven?"

"Yeah. Kids who aren't like me die."

The werewolf snapped, "None of that makes you an adult." His racing pulse triggered changes and, although he turned away to hide the gold in his eyes, he knew the child was close enough to catch an infinitesimal scent of wolf.

Jaylan's eyes widened. His brows arched under his dreadlocks. He pressed back into his seat and whispered, "Okay. Okay. Decompress . . . Uncle Devan."

"Let's get some sleep."

They slumped in the seat and Jaylan rested his head on the uncomfortable backpack. He slipped into a deep sleep while his father closed his eyes but remained alert.

At the train station, Jamaica—having hated the previous separation—insisted they be body-checked in the same booth. With his son's wide eyes staring at him, he worried that he had made a mistake.

On the train, Jaylan asked, "Was my dad as strong as you? Mom never mentioned it."

The pretender answered, "Twins, soldiers first then blue collar."

The boy closed his eyes and slept all the way to Miami, but Jamaica could not sleep. As passing zombies grated on the father's nerves, he wondered when and how he could tell his son that he was Jamaica, not Devan.

At the Miami station, disembarking train passengers who had no one picking them up boarded a shuttle. No one liked tight quarters and nearby strangers, and they shifted and leaned away from each other.

The driver, glaring into his rearview mirror shouted, "Relax people. You weren't infected on the train, so you're not infected here." He drove different couples and singles to different cars in a vast lot. Then he drove Jamaica and Jaylan to a two-year-old silver grey Toyota. Handing the father the keys, he said, "Bigger guy: bigger car, and it's a safer one for the kid."

Jamaica said, "Thank you," and the diver closed the shuttle doors and left. The werewolf turned to his son and said, "We're going south."

Jaylan slid into the car and said, "There should be a GPS, but there isn't one."

Jamaica said, "I have a portable one in my duffle.

The boy pulled it out and tried it. "Not working," he sighed.

"Check the glove compartment for a map."

Jaylan pulled one out and waved it before opening it.

Leaving the lot, Jamaica took a corner too fast and rammed into a zombie.

"Dented already!" Jaylan complained. Then he added, "Maybe I should drive."

Jamaica backed the car away, but the creature hung on. The werewolf zigzagged the car at high speed, slamming himself and his son against the doors.

The biter slid off the hood.

Jamaica shifted into reverse and began backing out of the street.

An explosion thundered within the car.

Jaylan, leaning out the open window, had fired a kill-shot. He screamed at the adult, "We can't leave him to attack someone else!"

Jamaica slammed on the breaks and shouted back, "I wanted to get you away from trouble."

Jaylan yelled, "There's no 'getting away' from trouble. There's only the next trouble!"

An old man shouted at them from a first floor window, "Hey! Where're you going?" He stroked the head of the infant on his lap. When Jamaica yelled that they wanted the Everglades, the old man shouted directions and ended with "Good luck!"

After calling, "Thank you," Jaylan swatted away flies before raising the window.

His father asked, "Can you see where 79th is on the map?"

"Yeah, the third left coming up."

After making the turn, Jamaica whispered, "What happened to your mother?"

Staring out the window, Jaylan murmured, "What else? She came home infected, so I put her down. That's what she taught me to do."

Shaken by the image of his young son killing his wife, Jamaica stopped talking.

Pulling a cell phone from his pocket, Jaylan made a call and said, "Hey, it's Jaylan. Yeah. I'm tope. Are you still hooked into the military and police bands? Good, Let them know we just took out a walking flesh bag on a Miami street near the train station. They need to know there might be more. Thanks."

When his son hung up, Jamaica asked, "Tope?"

Striking a cocky pose, the boy said, "Yeah, I'm better than fine."

"Military and police bands?"

"I know bloggers who know people."

The father suppressed his smile and kept driving. They found Route 1 and drove parallel to the ocean, until they passed a cement wall that enclosed a burned-out section of the city. Jamaica sniffed and said, "Napalm."

"You in the service?"

"As a young man."

The boy's voice dropped to just above a whisper and he said, "My father, too. Mom told me." At the mention of his mother, Jaylan turned toward the window.

The werewolf smelled his son's tears.

"I left her body in the apartment," the boy continued, "and never went back. The city—and Mom—are ashes, now."

In silence, they drove past a row of neat one-story cottages, followed by a sign for a cemetery.

"We should stop for food," Jamaica said.

"Not hungry."

"Doesn't matter. I see an orchard, so we're stopping. We don't know when we'll see another one."

They divided a dozen peaches between the father's duffle bag and his son's backpack. Further down the highway they passed a residential strip of pastel mansions with lawns that had gone to sand and weeds. Jamaica guessed the community survived by giving jobs and orphaned houses to refugees. Having families maintain and protect homes reduced the number of zombie nests.

Jamaica waved down a police car and asked, "Any safe place to eat?"

The police officer behind the wheel answered, "Go south another mile. Look for a billboard painted over with the word, 'Food,' and turn left."

Jamaica thanked her while Jaylan groaned, "They're going to charge you a year's rent for a glass of iced tea. We should just eat the fruit we found. Fruit on trees is free."

"We never know when food will be available, so we don't pass up a chance for more—even when we already have a little." He found the small, squat building with police cars in the large lot, and he parked.

Alongside the building, three generators cranked and three grills waited—all protected by armed guards. Laughter drifted from the windows.

Not wanting to leave their only possessions in the car, Jamaica carried his duffle and Jaylan his backpack into the restaurant. Inside the cool, dark space, a half dozen uniformed people swapped stories at a long bar. Seven patrons filled two of the dozen candle-lit tables. Some wore baseball caps and work boots. The rest wore cowboy hats and western boots.

Jamaica chose a table near a wall with a view of the other tables and the door. Jaylan sat next to him with his chair angled for the same view.

The server, in her early teens, smiled as she placed menus in front of them. Young, brunette, and on the heavy side, she measured Jaylan. "You're not from 'round here," she said, "or cops. Our usual customers are locals and cops." She nodded and added, "Last week, a military unit swept the area clean of zombies. Good thing they didn't stop to eat; we wouldn't have had enough food for everyone."

The small, elderly man behind the bar barked, "Rosie, you going to take their orders or talk them to death?"

"Okay, Grandpa, okay. It's just that I don't often see kids my age."

Jaylan grinned, saying, "It's all good. You want to slide into my DM?"

Jamaica gaped at his son.

The girl smiled and said, "Sure."

Jamaica's eyes widened, but the teenagers pulled out their cell phones and held them so they touched. After a series of chirps that sounded a little promiscuous to the father, the kids smiled at each other. The girl asked the werewolf, "What would you like, sir? We have red snapper, fresh off the boat this morning. Grandpa fries the best hush puppies and fat back. We also sweetened tea this morning."

Jamaica cut her off with, "Any beef?"

"We're all helping local farmers protect their herds, so—today—they gave us some ribs."

"I'll have ribs."

Jaylan cut in, saying, "I want the red snapper, but I need to know what all this will cost."

She flipped a receipt toward him, saying, "See. We're fair. The local power grid breaks down sometimes, and gas for the generators depends on what the locals can scavenge for us. Ice isn't easy to make. So, we have-tah sell all our food each day."

Jamaica handed her his card to swipe and assured her, "That'll be fine."

In-between taking care of patrons at the other tables, the girl texted Jaylan, who texted back. Both kids beamed.

She brought food to their table steaming with the different aromas.

After their meal, the father pulled his son away. They headed for their car with Jaylan still texting.

"Eyes up," Jamaica yelled.

Jaylan pocketed the cell phone and scanned the area around them.

Secured in the car, Jamaica asked, "Slide into my DM? What's that?"

"We're connecting. You know, Facebook, Instagram; the net's still wherever there's a working tower. You know why she smells so nice?"

"Please tell me you didn't ask her that."

"Her grandpa has a dozen rain barrels out back—not just one. She heats water on the grill to shampoo her hair and wash her clothes."

"You asked about her bathing?"

"No. She volunteered it. Then she said her grandfather would let us wash up."

Tempted, Jamaica still said, "No, we have to go."

The two found their way back to Route One to continue south. Burned skyscrapers crumbled behind the cement walls that bordered both sides of that stretch of the road. On a section of wall, someone had scrawled, "RIP, Cutler Bay."

On another billboard, someone had scrawled "Permanently Cancelled" over the words, "International Realtors Conference."

Jamaica had only driven a brief time before Jaylan yelled, "Shit!"

Jamaica slammed on the breaks.

Three alligators lay across the road.

"What do we do?" Jaylan asked.

Shaking his head, Jamaica said, "Not sure." He dried his sweaty palms on his jeans, and then rolled the car forward. The first alligator roared and clamped its jaws around the front bumper. Yanking its body side-to-side the 'gator pulled the bumper off the car. Backing away, the giant spiraled with the bumper, clanking metal against pavement with each twist.

Another alligator darted toward the first, taking hold of the bumper's other end. The two beasts twisted in opposite directions bending the metal with a shrill screech. As they tussled, Jamaica inched the car past them. The third creature twisted and went under the vehicle.

Raising his feet from the floorboards, Jaylan yelped, "Oh! Shit! It's under us!"

Jamaica, spotting it in the rearview mirror, said, "We're clear."

Jaylan checked the map and said, "Okay. We're good."

They soon came to a "Welcome to Homestead" sign. The next block gave them glimpses of the ocean between firebombed high-rise hotels and torched mansions. A half mile later modest homes had thriving gardens and manicured lawns. Small businesses had "open" signs in their windows, and armed citizens patrolled the neighborhood. Jamaica chose a guarded store where he used the pack's credit card to purchase water bottles and snacks. From Homestead, they headed west.

At a wide section of the C-111 canal, zombies crowded together on a bridge. Jamaica stopped the car. His chest tightened, and he gripped the steering wheel firm enough to fear the metal might bend. He shifted away from his son to hide his changing eyes and dropped his hands between his legs to hide his growing nails. With effort, he evened his breathing and restored his human condition. Then he said, "there are too many of them on that bridge. We can't drive through them."

"You think we're safer on foot?"

Looking at the canal, Jamaica said, "Zombies can't swim."

"Yeah, but alligators do."

"Let me borrow your phone."

Seeing his son's shudder, Jamaica promised, "I'm not running away, Jaylan."

Hesitant, the boy handed over the phone.

Jamaica dialed a number and said, "It's me. Find Keenu and tell her we need help. Okay. Thanks."

As he handed back the phone, Jaylan asked, "Now what?"

"Now, we wait."

"Who's Keenu?"

"She helped me and the others in Dohiyi."

"How the hell can she help us here?"

"Language, kid. Language."

Chapter 8

Jamaica's Return

In camp, Kristian found Keenu on a walkway, and said, "Excuse me."

"Yes?"

"Jamaica is trying to bring his son here and they need help. He's less than a day away from transforming and doesn't want to do that in front of Jaylan. Is there anything you can do?" Then he added, "If you can't help, our pack will go."

Facing the sun, she used a long fingernail to scratch at the screening she hated. Then she said, "Leave me and I'll do what I can."

Kristian went to find his wife and the other werewolves.

Keenu slipped under the screening and climbed down the ladder to the boat dock. On her knees, she extended her hands, palms down, over the water and intoned,

Mother of the seven seas,
Raise the images that I need.

The water churned and the likenesses of a man and a boy appeared on the surface. They sat in a car. Ahead of them, zombies crowded a bridge over a canal. In the water, alligators waited.

With one fingertip, Keenu touched the image without breaking it, and murmured,

With a power kind and cruel,
Make their water a whirlpool.
Man and boy in God's strong arms:
Turn all dangers with this charm.

She repeated the verse, and then said it two more times.

From the car, Jamaica and his son stared as the water whipped and coiled.

Jaylan blurted out, "What the hell is that?"

Jamaica did not answer.

A wind whirled until a funnel widened on their side of the canal.

"What is that?" Jaylan demanded.

Jamaica gunned the engine and brought the car alongside the edge of the canal.

"What are you doing?"

"Grab your pack and let's go."

"Uh-uh. No way!"

With the strength of his wolf, the terrified father pulled the boy from the car, shouting, "Let's go. Now!"

As the spinning water nicked the embankment, Jamaica lowered his trembling son over the side of the whirlpool onto the sand at its center. Then he jumped in and took hold of the boy to steady him. The water churned around them, casting alligators to the other side of a liquid barrier.

Jaylan, struggling against his father's grip, shouted, "Alligators breathe air, man. They can poke right through that water."

Jamaica growled, "Walk or be carried, but we're going."

The wind deafened them. Alligators that slapped against the barrier were spun away. The vortex churned across the canal. Jaylan and his father staggered forward within it.

Having crossed the canal, the whirlpool nicked the far embankment. Jamaica lifted his son over its rim and leapt for a fingerhold. The dirt crumbled, Years before, during the construction of the canal, workers had packed and mounded spoiled dirt to make an embankment. Jamaica snatched another handhold, but the loose soil gave way.

Jaylan grabbed his father's shirt and pulled it. The boy's determination helped the big man over the edge.

The funnel dissipated, and the wind carried one thought: "Climb."

Jamaica scooped Jaylan under one arm and reached for a tree limb with the other. He pulled his son with him onto a fork and they leaned against the trunk. The werewolf glanced at approaching zombies and snarled, "We aren't high enough. Climb. Go!"

Jaylan climbed but slipped. Jamaica caught him, lifted him higher, and steadied him while zombies reached the tree and clawed at the trunk.

The boy shouted, "What the fuck was that?"

Not knowing a better way to say it, Jamaica blurted out, "You believe in zombies?"

Glancing below, Jaylan glared at the man in front of him.

"Then believe in witches."

Back in camp, Keenu, still kneeling on the dock, touched the air with one hand and intoned,

Wind bend trees one to another.
Branches weave into each other.
Strong bridges made from leafy domes:
Help our brave friends come safely home.

In the tree, Jaylan did not have time to question the existence of witches before the wind rose and the tree groaned. Father and son hung on tight while their perch creaked and twisted. Then, every tree ahead of them entwined their branches.

"Let's go," Jamaica said.

"Go?"

"Now!"

Jamaica nudged Jaylan forward to where their tree interlocked with the next and urged him across.

Below them, putrid mouths opened, and boney hands clawed the air.

Light-headed, Jaylan swayed.

His father grabbed the back of his shirt, steadied him, and said, "Rest a moment, and stop looking down."

Jamaica stared at the twilight sky and began to perspire. He shuddered with the effort to contain the wolf that threatened to emerge.

A barrage of gunfire startled them.

"It's okay," Jamaica assured his son, "That's coming from the front barrier of the camp. We're approaching from the side."

In camp, Kristian worried about the witch having spent hours on her knees crooning her spells. He whispered to his wife, "Find the witch's daughter."

Mary took off at a full run, and soon returned with Alexandria.

Kristian pointed toward the ladder and said, "Your mother's been trying to save a werewolf and his son. I'm worried about her."

Alexandria nodded and went to the edge of the walkway above the ladder. Knowing not to interrupt her mother, she climbed down to the middle rung and closed her eyes. In her mind, the images formed of a man and boy picking their way from tree limb to tree limb above a herd of snarling biters. The daughter murmured incantations to add her strength to her mother's.

Jamaica and Jaylan reached the perimeter at the same time Alexandria called to the alpha wolf, "Mama's done. Help her."

Kristian descended the ladder and helped the witch climb to the walkway and helped Keenu to her tent.

On the west edge of camp, guards wrapped the travelers in blankets and led them to the field hospital.

There, a physician tended to the silent boy's cuts and scrapes.

As soon as the staff left their new patient resting, Jamaica approached Jaylan's cot and said, "I have to leave you while I report to Sergeant Schwinn."

"Leaving me? I said this is a sucky rescue!"

His father, struggling against the coming change, snarled at the staff, "My name is Devan. That's my nephew." Never having treated him for wounds, and never having fought beside him, the staff did not remember him from Dohiyi.

Chapter 9

Shallow Waters

As Ritt and Keenu watched the guide boats maneuver into position, Keenu dragged her long, emerald nails across the screens complaining, "To help the vampires, the rest of us are separated from the sun?"

"We have platforms and lawns without roofs or screens."

"Not enough," she complained.

The sunset created an amber halo around the witch's skin and her hazel eyes glinted. Their clothing ruffled in an aberrant breeze that also stirred the water and pushed alligator hatchings farther from the pier. Above the Marine and the witch, branches bent, and clouds billowed.

Ritt assured her, "The roofs and netting are better for my people, too. They're protection from the sun and the mosquitos."

She closed her eyes and breathed more easily. The wind dissipated. "I'm sorry," she said, "but the vampires and werewolves make me edgy."

"All of you make me edgy."

An explosion of gunfire from the perimeter vibrated the walkway. The guards were a thin line between camp and herds of biters.

Thinking about the death of her daughter, Linett, the witch's anger toward Avianna and Hilanor festered. Controlling her emotions, she asked the Lieutenant, "How do you intend to use Missy and Alexandria?"

Ritt remembered that precautions had not saved two of his Marines from rotters in Dohiyi but, forcing confidence into his voice, he said, "I'll keep them in the helicopters, Miss Keenu. We gave them better cameras and communications. They can film from a safe distance and they can also blog."

Keenu nodded.

Ritt remembered the lovely Linett in Dohiyi. Bringing his mind to the present, he watched the witch walk toward the two-room tent she shared with the wizard. As Keenu passed the parade of vampires, she gave them only a brief and chilly glance.

Below their shaved pates, the samurai's long braids hung down their backs and their white long-sleeved shirts were tucked into black hitatare trousers. They carried thirty-inch curved katanas and eighteen-inch Wakizashis in sheaths on their belts and had six-foot long Bo-jutsu staffs strapped to their backs.

Avianna and Joseph, wearing army-issued black jumpsuits, followed the samurai. Avianna wore a katana strapped to her back and a sheathed Wakizashi hung from her belt. Joseph wore only a sheathed knife on his belt.

Behind Avianna and Joseph, Ulric wore a holstered a Colt 45 and a sheathed Civil War officer's sword hung from his belt.

All five vampires took places beside the Lieutenant the water's edge and donned their hooded capes and gloves.

Along the tree line, the water reflected the dark green overhanging foliage. In the center of the canal, the water mirrored the blue sky. Arrays of lilies floated far enough from each other to create avenues in between.

A hornet sound, increasing in volume, announced the approach of airboats.

As the crafts docked, Avianna, Joseph, and Ulric boarded one, the samurai in a second, and the witch and wizard boarded a third and a fourth. Once Marines boarded the airboats, the vessels followed guide boats out of the channel and into open water. There, the armada slowed enough to scan different hammocks for biters.

A stocky Marine shouted to the others, "Where the hell are all the zombies and refugees that are supposed to fill the 'glades?"

A taller Marine pointed toward alligators sunning themselves on a nearby bank, and said, "There's part of your answer."

As the airboat carrying Avianna, Joseph, and Ulric pulled alongside an island, their Marines took down zombies at the water's edge. Then the vampires leapt from the boats onto the tangle of tree roots.

A local in a guide boat called, "Careful! That muck's a tangle of trunks, and roots, and sludge."

Another one called, "There can be alligators down there, too."

The first one yelled, "Oh, yeah, and water snakes and leeches. Welcome to our 'glades!"

Stepping on the tangled roots, Avianna slid her lean body around under a pond apple tree's low branches. Joseph, not as flexible or quick, moved with more care than his mate. Ulric, not wanting her to best him, charged through branches, still outdistanced by the graceful she-vamp.

Avianna stopped short of the grasping hands of a jaw-snapping biter. The zombie had been snagged on a broken branch for so long that vines had ensnared him. He might have been thirty-years-old when a bite stopped his aging. He wore pseudo-camo fishing vest. A plastic pike with hooks and a sixteen-inch rubber worm hung from his pockets. A spider, with a red head and legs, and a black abdomen crawled across his neck. Avianna climbed to a branch above the rotter and drew her Wakizashi. Gripping the intricate weave around the handle, she drove the knife through the top of the biter's head.

Joseph stood on a large vine. Nearby a dozen short pond-apple trees clustered; moss hung from them like clothing on a line. A cacophony of bird and insect sounds accompanied the grunts of approaching zombies. Water splashed his feet as a bloated creature rose to the surface, reaching for him. Joseph draped his body over a heavy limb and extended both arms downward. With one powerful twist, he removed the creature's head, and dropped it into the muck.

Ulric, seeing what Joseph had done, took note of the man's strength. Distracted, he did not see the python until it wrapped itself around his leg and sunk its fangs deep into his thigh. Ignoring the pain, Ulric grabbed the thick snake where its jaws hinged. He forced open the reptilian mouth, wider and wider, until the jaw snapped. Then he separated the head from the body and unwound the eleven-foot snake from his leg and the trunk of the palm tree. Ulric pushed the wounded leg forward to show the others his bleeding wound and held up the dead python to illustrate his strength.

Avianna and Joseph did not see it.

Joseph, standing on the roots of a mangrove tree, wrestled with a zombie a foot taller and a hundred pounds heavier than himself. He pushed his attacker backward and leapt into a Mangrove tree. The zombie reached for him, and the vampire drove the blade of his hunting knife into the biter's skull. When he pulled back his weapon, the creature slumped into the roots.

Avianna, balancing on the bend of a tree trunk, and bending low over the water, reached out with both hands. She straightened, holding what looked like a roll of soggy rags. Slow and gentle, Avianna unwrapped the bundling to reveal a baby. Ignoring the fighting around her, she held the little one at arms-length. The once adorable face had grayed and dried. Avianna checked the infant for wounds. Finding none, she smoothed the yellow dress, cradled the bundle, and murmured, "*Dolce bambina.* They intended to come back for you, yes? How you must have waited. How you must have cried."

A sound behind Avianna spun her toward the biter who reached for her. Still cradling the bundle in one arm, she drew her Wakizashi with her free hand and sliced through the old rotter.

Ulric watched Avianna's striking arm change into mist and pass around a thick branch. It coalesced on the other side and continued its swing. When Ulric shape-shifted into a bat, mist, or wolf, he transformed entirely. Never having seen another vampire mist only one body part, he shuddered at her powers.

Pointing at something, Joseph shouted, "Ulric!"

Ulric twisted to find a biter reaching for him. Only traces of her youthful beauty and coppery hair remained. Ulric grabbed the sides of her head, but she kept snapping. Ulric's quick twist removed her head, letting the torso drop among the tangled roots. He dropped the head to the muck below and rotated to find Avianna still cradling the infant she had found. "What are you doing with that?" he yelled.

In soothing tones, Joseph queried, "Avianna?"

Looking down at the fish-filled mire and up into the bird-filled trees, she murmured, "*Mi dispiace,* little one."

Joseph urged, "Avianna, I understand 'sorry,' but you must let her go."

The vampire who would never have a child of her own, rewrapped the baby with a tenderness that shocked Ulric. Then she leaned over the water to reposition the bundle in the tangle of roots.

A mile away, Akio and Isamu perched in a torchwood tree above a half-dozen rotters, all clawing upward. The taller, leaner Isamu moved gracefully from limb to limb. The shorter Akio powered through the branches. Believing that they freed innocent spirits from damnation, the brothers delivered one-strike dénouements to the afflicted creatures below them.

Akio slid away from a brown recluse spider. The insect's poison would not cost the vampire a limb, but a poisoned muscle would slow him down.

In the airboats, Marines shot the zombies within range. One said, "Wow! Look at how those vampires move!"

Another answered, "Yeah. Look closely because we'll be fighting them someday."

Eyes narrowed, face drawn, the first did not respond.

***

Keenu focused on the pythons and alligators that crowded the different crafts.

Butting an alligator head with the butt of his weapon, a Marine complained, "A biter diet has made them too damn used to eating humans."

Afraid that blood in the water would trigger a feeding frenzy, warriors on the boats used weapons to jab at the alligators' eyes and slap the water's surface to drive back the snakes.

Keenu gazed into the shallow water. Its warmth became her warmth. Life under the water's surface pulsed within the witch and she intoned,

Mother of these gentle waves
Make the water not a grave.
Move each approaching threat
And send it to the muddy bed.

As the water spiraled, green dragonflies with black banded tails lifted off the water and fled. Thrashing alligators and pythons, pulled to the bottom, breathed within giant air bubbles.

A quarter mile away, Marines shot zombies that clawed at a chickee. The chickee wobbled under the attack. The family on the platform, two adults cradled three children. They clung to each other and cried.

In a boat nearby, Hilanor touched the water with the tip of his staff. Connecting to the heavenly source of his power, the old wizard shouted,

Wood that creaks and wood that groans.
Lives depend upon your bones.
Stand straight and strong. Those
Sweet lives to prolong.

The water around his staff flowed toward the weakening chickee. When the ripples touched the wood, the posts steadied and held firm. A volley of shots exploded from Marine guns, and the infected creatures fell to approaching alligators. The deadly frenzy made even the hardened witnesses cringe.

Chapter 10

Werewolves and Swampbuggies

The Lieutenant found Keenu alone by the railing and, without preamble, said, "I need your help with the werewolves. I need them to stay wolves for the rest of our time here."

Eyes wide and voice tremorous, she said, "You don't know what you're asking. Subverting the will or changing the body in a sentient being takes dark magic."

He softened his voice to say, "It's necessary. I already spoke to them."

"Not good enough! I must talk to the werewolves myself, and to Hilanor, and to my coven."

"Please do it soon. They need to go on patrol in wolf form."

She nodded and left him to find Kristian.

The alphas and the other werewolves sat outside their tents, drinking beer, and laughing.

She stepped into their circle and said, "You spoke to the Lieutenant and know what he wants me to do?"

Mary answered, "We're the ones who suggested it."

"In human form," Kristian added, "we're stronger and faster than other humans; but, as wolves, we have full speed and heightened senses."

Jamaica explained, "We've evolved enough that we can transform two days before and two days after the full moon. It was enough in Dohiyi, but not enough for how long we'll be here."

Keenu asked Elderwolf and Girl, "Do you agree?"

"Yes, ma'am" they chorused.

"And if I can't change you back? If you stay wolves? Jamaica, think of your son."

He had no answer.

"What if the spell erases your humanity and you become feral—feral with werewolf strength and speed? What if you turn on the Marines?"

Kristian held Mary's hand while answering, "Then, they use their silver bullets; we know they have them."

In her toughest 'mom' voice, she said, "I need to think—and, Jamaica, you need to tell Jaylan who and what you are before someone else does—or before your son sees you change. It's lies that killed my Linett. . .twice! Tell Jaylan!"

Jamaica said nothing.

The witch scowled at him for another minute before going to the tent she shared with Hilanor.

The old wizard greeted her with, "I know why you're here. We must try."

"It's dark magic, my friend."

He rested a gnarled hand on her shoulder and said, "It's true that dark magic can change a white witch, but you didn't change when you cast the spell on Avianna's sire."

Keenu shook her head and answered, "But Kahl-maus was already dead. He had already killed a Marine. Both Avianna and Joseph were willing to risk their destruction if my spell went wrong. Kahl-maus also made his misting appear as smoke to terrify people. All of that made the decision to use dark magic easier. It's different with Kristian's and Mary's pack." She shook her head and added, "They are alive and with families. They hunt animals instead of humans. I don't want to risk locking them in that form forever."

"You must trust your magic, and your coven."

Keenu's hand trembled as she pulled her cell phone from her pocket and dialed.

The wiccan who answered listed to Keenu's lengthy explanation, and then called a meeting of the coven. The women spent the evening gathering supplies for the next day and then resting.

Hilanor and Keenu knew that a wrong word could spin dark forces in an unwanted direction. To avoid error, they wrote and rewrote the spell. "I'm a terrible poet," Keenu groaned.

"Use the right words and nature will respond."

The next morning, the coven gathered in the village meeting room. They burned rosemary and saffron to help the werewolves remember their humanity; chamomile to ease their stress, peppermint, ginger, and turmeric to ease any agony the spell might cause them.

In camp, sitting by the helicopters, the witch and the wizard wore ceremonial black robes and knelt in a circle of candles. On the ground between them, they lay five small sticks.

In the meeting house in the witch's village, the coven laid on an alter cloth the dolls that represented the wolves. An incantation murmured by the witch and the coven bound Keenu's sticks and the coven's dolls to the living wolves they represented.

Keenu and Hilanor waved smoking bundles of dried sage and citronella around themselves and over the sticks while the coven did the same with the dolls.

Hilanor knelt on the ground and closed his eyes. The old wizard and the distant coven drew strength from the energies around them. Keenu drew power from the sun above and intoned:

Loving God of wolf and man,
Bind these five, their paws to hand.
In our need and for this time:
In their eyes a full moon shines.

When my blood calls for an end,
Let them know each phase again.

Keenu stood and stumbled. She sat again. Hilanor, still on the ground, put his arms around her.

In the treehouse meeting room, the eyes of the five wolf-shaped dolls flared red before returning to normal. Members of the coven struggled with their fears and fatigue. One of them mumbled, "This is worse than when we helped Keenu lock the vampire into his illusion. This time, it was harder to pull Keenu back from the darkness she invoked."

Other's in the circle nodded, but no one spoke. From the corner of the room, the black cat, Merlin, watched with golden eyes.

In their tent, the werewolves endured their twisting, bone-breaking transformations into wolves. They screamed and howled through it all. Afterward, they lie panting and trembling for fifteen minutes before being able to stand.

The three-hundred-and-fifty-pound white alpha, Kristian, and his slightly smaller wife Mary nuzzled each other. The gray Elderwolf checked over the youngest and smallest wolf—the two-hundred-and-fifty-pound Girl. Jamaica, the black beta, and the pack's largest wolf stood apart from the others.

Kristian howled and the five ran from the tent.

***

Outside the western wall, Sergeant Benwahr's people provided cover while Sergeant Max Schwinn's squad gathered near three swampbuggies. The squad, comprised of Schwinn as leader and three fire-teams of four Marines each, examined the vehicles. Seats were perched on open platforms, with railings around the edges. Each rig squatted on oversized tires. Schwinn grunted, "I don't like the exposure."

In the clearing, Schwinn's squad loaded gear onto the buggies. When the wolves arrived and the vehicles were loaded, Schwinn called for everyone's attention. He said to his people, "You learned to work with supernaturals in Dohiyi, but the witch has changed something. The werewolves will now scout for us in wolf form no matter how long we're here." To the wolves, he said, "We don't know if you can be infected, so I want you to drop back from zombie herds. Understood? The last thing we need is a zombie werewolf!"

In unison, the five wolves lowered their heads.

"Okay, everyone on board."

Mary and Kristian leapt onto the Sportsman. Jamaica and Elderwolf jumped onto the Explorer. Girl and Schwinn boarded the Scout. The Marines, in their teams, divided among the buggies. Then the vehicles rolled forward, bouncing along a muddy trail through the bog.

The Marines tried to detect the approach of zombies through the cacophony of Cricket Frogs croaking, Pig Frogs hooting like owls, birds calling, and the songs of thousands of insects. They tried to smell biters through the mix of rotting underwater vegetation and the fragrances of Sweetbay Magnolias and White Swamp Lilies. The overgrowth along the neglected trail brushed against the sides of the vehicles and the combatants became hyper-aware of every movement.

On the Explorer, Elderwolf circled in place. He loved Girl like a daughter and regretted separating. He would have paced along the railing if Jamaica had not blocked his path.

The Scout's old engine screeched and whined. The young wolf scratched her ears, quivered, whimpered, and paced on the narrow passage between the seats and the boat's edge.

One of the Marines, an eighteen-year-old, nicknamed Witt, grumbled: "Can you stop pacin'? You're making me as nervous as bait on a hook."

The young wolf came nose to nose with the Marine and bared her long canines. Saliva dripped from her retracted gums onto his knees. She considered snarling, but his having four other armed Marines with him changed her mind. With her hazel eyes narrowed and her ears back she studied them.

Witt exhaled, "Okay. Okay. Go on an' pace if that'll dill your pickle."

With the Marine's words still hanging in the air, the werewolf spun away. The wolf, who easily separated dozens of different smells in the sawgrass, water, and trees, lifted her nose and straightened her ears. She and the wolves on the other vehicles howled in unison and leapt over the railings of the moving vehicles.

While the adult wolves held their ground, pointing and snarling toward the palm trees, Girl darted in through the shrubs.

Schwinn radioed the drivers to stop the buggies and told his team leaders to disembark their people. The soldiers clambered down just as Girl yelped and cried. Her pack darted into the forest.

Schwinn yelled to a team leader, "Go after them—but be careful!"

The four-man team rushed, without running, into the brush.

Witt was the first one to arrive at the chaotic scene and stopped short, unsure what to do.

The young wolf stood with her jaws stretched around a fifteen-foot Burmese Python, just above its trachea. The snake had coiled around Girl's body and was squeezing. The other wolves bit and pulled at the reptile, but it would not loosen its grip.

Witt pushed through the pack, yelling, "Let me in there!" He dropped to his knees beside Girl. Leaning away from the snake's head, he pulled out his knife and yanked a gouged and bleeding part of the snake away from the young wolf. Yelling, "Shit! Shit! Shit!' he slipped his knife between the reptile and wolf and sliced at the underside of the snake.

The snakes head drooped to the ground and the coiling stopped, but the python's muscles remained tight around the young wolf.

Girl, with her head hanging, tongue out, and eyes rolling back stopped breathing. As she collapsed, the other wolves lunged forward and ripped away chunks of the snake.

Witt pulled at the reptilian body wherever the wolves had done the most damage and sections of the snake came off in the mouths of the wolves and the hands of the Marine until they freed Girl.

Witt checked the young wolf then yelled, "Come on, Girl. Breathe!" He raised her snout, held her mouth closed, and breathed into her nose. He repeated the rhythm until her chest rose and she expelled air. Then he leaned back, watching the other wolves remove all remnants of the snake from their panting friend.

"Well done," Schwinn said from behind Witt, and the Marine realized the squad had encircled himself and the wolves.

An older Marine said, "So, I guess that-there's a first kiss for you two."

"Knock it off," Witt snapped, "When she's people, she's about fifteen!"

The squad's laughter brought the wolf to full awareness. Shaky and bruised, Girl pushed herself into a standing position and shook off the muck and grass.

Without a moment's rest, all the wolves spun at the same time and snarled toward the forest north of them.

Schwinn yelled, "Heads up!"

Grunts and the stench of death came from behind the nearest tree line.

It was too late to use the wedge formation that Schwinn had planned for the limited visibility and close terrain, so he ordered, "Form a line! Arms-length apart!"

The Marines, with tight chests and pounding hearts, did as ordered. Marco Coraggio and Creole Vanyan, Schwinn's best sharpshooters, stood with the other warriors. Marco's straight, black hair escaped his helmet. Creole's dark skin glistened with perspiration.

Near the line, the wolves stood guard: Mary and Kristian in front, Jamaica to the east, Elderwolf to the west, and Girl behind the line, watching the rear.

Zombies emerged from the forest as though parting curtains. Two of the females wore tattered dresses with hats trimmed in red flowers and feathers. Others wore a mix of office clothing or hunting and fishing gear.

"Wolves to the rear!" Schwinn yelled, "And don't fuckin' get bit!"

Mary and Kristian led their pack members behind the Marines' line, but the wolves would not leave their squad.

One of the men shook his head and grumbled, "Damn. There's kids with them."

Raising his rifle, the Marine to his right said, "They're already dead! We're not killin' nothin'." She fired, and a child, still in her pink pajamas, fell into the peat that covered the limestone bed.

On the left end of the line, a Marine who had been focusing on the herd ahead was grabbed from the side. The young warrior swiveled and slammed the butt of her rifle into the biter's head. The zombie stumbled backward and the Marine fired and dropped him.

As waves of biter's staggered into the Marine assault, one fell close to Witt. Firing in a different direction, the young fighter had not seen him.

Jamaica leapt forward and grabbed hold of the zombie's shirt. The huge wolf yanked the rotter away from Witt, who blasted the zombie, and said, "Thanks," to the wolf.

On the other side of the line, a bitter fell close enough to grab the leg of a Marine. Not wanting to shoot himself, the man crushed the zombie's head with the butt of his rifle, and then he pulled it's jaw away from his bloody pants leg.

Elderwolf ran through the fray to the wounded Marine. He sniffed his leg, whined, and then tugged on the man's shirt.

The Marine yelled, "Knock it off! Let me go! I can still fight." When the man's shirt tore, the wolf grabbed his uninjured leg and pulled him off balance, and then dragged him by his collar toward the back of the line. The commotion caught the attention of the two nearest Marines, who grabbed and half-carried their comrade back to the buggies.

As the wounded man's carriers returned to the skirmish, a driver rushed to him with a first aid kit, and another radioed for a helo to airlift the wounded Marine to base.

"You know I only have about twenty more minutes," the injured man yelled. Grabbing the collar of his attendant he screamed, "So chop it off!"

"In the helo. They'll have the tools in the helo."

"My mind will already be gone."

Above them, the winds from a descending medevac stirred treetops and scattered debris on the ground. Medics dropped a stretcher on ropes.

As they secured the wounded man, he screamed, "I only have ten minutes left. Cut it off!"

A medic from the helo promised, "In the helo. We can do it in the helo."

Medics raised the wounded man. The departing chopper whipped trees and shrubbery, obstructing the firing line's aim. Coraggio and Vanyan still dropped more zombies than the rest of the team, but waves of biters kept coming.

Seeing the wolves mixing in with his people and the zombies, Schwinn cursed then shouted, "Wolves to the buggies—now!" To his people, he yelled, "Back up! Back up! Shoot the biters' knees! Take them down! Take them all down!"

The Marines backed away, raking the area at knee level, forcing the last waves of the herd to the ground. Schwinn, remembering Anton Babineau—bitten in Dohiyi by a zombie lying under other bodies— yelled, "Watch for movement! Remember Anton!"

Into his CommLink, Schwinn called for air support.

The Marines, taking short breaths of the humid air, clipped bayonets to the ends of their weapons. Retreating, they fired at incoming stragglers and head-pierced the biters who fell close to them.

Schwinn, hearing the Blackhawk, called, "Evacuate! Evacuate! Everyone back to the buggies."

At the buggies, he asked a driver, "Where are the white wolves?"

"I asked them to stop the vultures from ripping the tires, and they carried the birds into the shrub."

Schwinn screamed, "Mary, Kristian, get back here!"

The Marines hunkered down under the buggies. The werewolves formed protective barriers between the fighters and anything that might come. The white wolves lie in front of Marco and Creole: the Marines who had covered their retreat in Dohiyi.

Engine roaring, blades whirling, the Blackhawk swooped low and raked the area then repeated the action. When it angled and flew off, Schwinn ordered his teams to, "Stack and burn the bodies!" Haunted by Anton, he repeated, "And be careful!"

Chapter 11

Resident Enemy

Inside the hospital, Joseph recognized the chaplain as the only member of the Dohiyi medical team to approach his kind.

"Are you injured?" the man asked.

Joseph explained, "No. I'm a surgeon and I heard you have a wounded Marine here. I want to see him."

A tall, blond, middle-aged man, standing on the other side of the room, interrupted with, "I'm his doctor, and I don't want your voodoo."

Without Avianna's wit, Joseph said, "I'm not giving you a choice."

The medical staff backed away from the vampire.

The wounded man on the gurney, having fought beside the supernaturals throughout the war, did not show fear.

"How're you doing, Marine?" Joseph asked.

Pale and perspiring, the young man gasped between words, "Will…I…heal?"

Joseph examined the patient and counted the beats of the young warrior's struggling heart. Concerned, he unwrapped the stump of the patient's leg. The doctors had tied off vessels, clamped arteries, and cauterized the wound without stopping the infection that already touched the warrior's brain and affected his speech.

"What think?" The wounded man asked.

Joseph reached into his patient's mind. He eased the man's fears and blocked the warrior's awareness of his pain.

The wounded Marine's eyes closed. His breathing steadied.

Joseph assured him, "I'll visit you again in a little while." Then he approached the chief physician and said, "He'll rest better now."

"Vampire, you had no right to mess with that man's mind."

"That's 'Doctor' to you, and your accessible mind."

Outside, Joseph found Avianna waiting for him. He knew she would have heard everything said inside.

She hugged him and whispered in his ear, "Are you going to kill him, to save him from experimentation in Aberdeen?"

"I'm considering it."

She pulled back but not out of his arms. Lowering her voice thickened her accent as she said, "If his mind were clear, he would volunteer for Aberdeen."

Henry's voice came from behind them, "Want my opinion—as a soldier?"

Avianna and Joseph separated and faced the other vampire without saying yes or no.

He answered his own question: "The man was brave in life. Allow him to be brave in death. Let him finish his mission." Blue veins showed under his pallid skin and his eyeteeth lengthened. "Everyone," he insisted, "must keep her word."

Without seeming to move, Avianna closed the gap between them. Staring into his eyes, she did not bare her fangs. In a deep, hardened voice she said, "I do not need lessons in honor."

Joseph yelled, "What in Hell is going on between you two?"

After Henry retracted his fangs and his skin returned to opaque, he answered, "We just have short fuses, your girlfriend and I."

Joseph frowned at Avianna.

She blocked Joseph from reading her thoughts but took his hand. "*Per favore, mi amore.* I am ready to be done with this world for today. *Per favore, mi amore.* Come to our tent with me."

He nodded and they walked away, leaving Henry staring after them.

In the tent, while they lie in each other's arms, Joseph said, "You are hiding something from me—something about Henry or Ulric, whatever his name is. I don't like it, Avianna."

"I met him a century ago, before he started using the name Ulric. I did not like him then or now."

"So, why bring him here?"

"He came to me."

"You brought him because you still don't think I'm strong enough."

She embraced Joseph and whispered, "Henry is a soldier and a vampire. I agreed to let him come because he can help the humans."

Still not believing she had shared the entire truth, he held her, kissed her, and yielded to the desire that inflamed them.

The next morning, Avianna scowled at the sun's glow through the canvas. Groaning, she rolled over and covered her face with the blanket.

Joseph stirred beside her, murmuring, "Hmm?"

"Again, we risk burning for the humans who will turn on us as soon as they think our help is unnecessary."

"True, but for my human family, I will keep helping."

Avianna rose and Joseph did as well. They dressed and went to the field hospital to use its equipment. Avianna warmed a blood bank donation. Crinkling her nose, she poured the red liquid into the crystal goblet she had brought from home. Joseph warmed the cow's blood that Ritt reserved for him.

While pretending to ignore the vampires' preparations, the disgust of the humans present washed over Avianna and Joseph like ice water.

Joseph checked his now unconscious patient, while Avianna's attention turned toward a young boy lying on a cot.

He tossed and turned, before settling onto his back and staring at the ceiling. In a whisper that no one should have heard, he grumbled, 'First zombies then witches now vampires. Where the fuck did my uncle bring me?' Then he shuddered.

Avianna approached the side of his cot and whispered so only the boy could hear, "I did not want to rejoin the coalition, but--like you—I am here for someone else." Then she purred, "But you and I, young warrior— shall make the best of it, because they were right to bring us."

As she and Joseph left the tent, she glanced back at the boy who sat watching her.

"Someone you know?" Joseph asked her.

"Me at that age, my love; only me."

Chapter 12

Airborne Reporters

Alexandria sat in her room going through the few photos she had taken of the Marines that day. She made notes for each one to give to Missy for her report. The duo trusted the bloggers who had been releasing their stories since the beginning of the infection. They also turned down money offered by a large newspaper.

Missy, pink with excitement, burst into their room shouting, "Let's go. They want us ready."

Pale and quivering, Alexandria shook her head.

Missy asked, "Have you had a vision?"

"No."

"Then let's go."

On the camp's helipad, the crew ran through the preflight check and loaded weaponry and parachutes, ammo, supplies, and gear. After a briefing, the crew helped Missy and Alexandria into their flight suits and helmets.

As they boarded, Alexandria's stomach knotted. She lacked her mother's intimacy with nature and worried that her under-developed, intermittent precognition would fail. The more she dwelled on her inadequacies, the less she wanted to be in the air. The crew's waterproof side arms reminded her that a fall into the water was possible.

She stuffed herself into the seat nearest the gunner and open door. Her flight suit bulged around the straps. Her long, thick curls pressed against the inside of the helmet, and she perspired in the insufferable heat. She glanced at Missy and groaned.

Missy's flight suit was a fashion statement. Wisps of the girl's wavy blonde hair escaped her helmet to play in the wind. Despite her being in the middle of the row, the sun haloed her lovely face.

On each side of the craft, a gunner pointed his weapon out his window. Between them, the passengers faced forward. Alexandria pulled her camera from her tote bag and Missy took a notebook from her backpack. The helicopter rose and wavered, and then it lifted higher before going forward.

Below them, the water mirrored cumulus clouds. Grass islands flattened into pieces on a vast puzzle board. Airboats, like toys in a bathtub, weaved through the channels.

Alexandria aimed her camera then trembled. She dropped it into her lap, murmuring, "No. No. No."

The pilot called back, "What?"

Alexandria yelled, "Go back! Land, now!"

The co-pilot did not react, but the pilot yelled, "Why?"

Alexandria closed her eyes. Holding her head, she repeated, "No. No. No."

Missy yelled to the pilot, "She sees something!" To Alexandria, she called, "What do you see?"

"A biter. A crash. Sex. Birds. Snapshots."

Missy yelled at the pilot, "Listen to her! Land!"

The pilot put the Blackhawk into a descent.

The co-pilot turned toward the pilot as though he had something to say. When she faced him, he grabbed and yanked her arm. Chomping and snarling from within his helmet burst through the comm system.

The struggling pilot could not break the new zombie's grip. The Blackhawk zigzagged. Blades whipped. The motor screamed. The craft tilted.

Doubled-over by a headache, Alexandria saw only her visions.

Water rippled around the growing grass islands. The gunnery Sergeant pulled his sidearm, placed the barrel against the co-pilot's helmet, and ended his friend's suffering. The bullet punctured the Blackhawk's windshield.

Events jumbled. A flock of cranes in its path collided with the chopper. The punctured glass shattered, and the wind lashed the crew and passengers with feathers and gore. Birds hit the tail rotor assembly, fragmenting the blades.

The pilot yelled through her mic, "We need a run-on landing. Look for a road or a long stretch of grass."

Peering past the gunnery Sergeant to her right and out the door, Missy yelled, "Why?"

The Gunnery Sergeant yelled back, "Slowing down will spin us. We need to fly straight and fast onto an open strip."

The pilot aimed the aircraft toward a path where the grass poked through the water's surface. With the vertical stabilizers damaged, the craft vibrated and rattled.

Alexandria gripped her head in two hands muttering, "Mama, help us."

The witch whispered in the girl's mind, "Trust. Believe. Know yourself."

Missy's body whipped to the side and her helmet banged against Alexandria's shoulder. Gripping her notepad with both hands she gasped at the marshland rushing toward them.

Outside one window, white clouds rose. Below another window, the smooth surface of the water reflected the falling aircraft. Missy hugged her pad to her chest. She licked her lips and tasted tears.

The lilting helicopter cut through screeching wildlife. Roots tore off the landing gear and shredded the craft's belly. The craft listed, careened left, and rolled onto its right side. Inside, the co-pilot went under water while the pilot dangled sideways in her harness. The Gunnery Sergeant to Missy's right sunk face down in the muck while water covered Missy and her notepad. Alexandria dangled from her seat harness, while the crew chief to her left slumped sideways against her.

Shock froze them all.

Then, everyone began stirring.

The crew chief freed himself and dropped the pilot's seat backward to give her support while she unbuckled.

Alexandria released her camera and grabbed Missy's flight suit to pull her above water. She screamed, "Missy, undo your belt!"

Missy, choking on a swill of feathers and bloody water, undid her buckle.

The gunny, with muck in his eyes and choking on water, unstrapped himself and rose.

As the crew and reporters struggled for footing in the shifting craft, a cottonmouth slid inside with a stream of water. The snake was longer and fatter than the ones Alexandria had seen near her mother's village. When it came close, it brought the stench of skunk.

The pilot drew her weapon and fired at the serpent's swerving head. She missed.

Alexandria called to her mother in a silent scream. Air, sweeping through cracks in the Blackhawk, spun the cottonmouth in a circle.

A new current took the snake out the crew chief's door, as the head and upper torso of a zombie filled the opening. Tall and broad, with glazed eyes, a slack jaw, and rotting skin, it snarled and stumbled into the shifting craft.

The crew chief, with his gun still drawn, aimed, and fired. He did not miss. Brain matter splattered everyone.

Alexandria, covered in muck, regained her senses to announce, "We're going to be okay, now."

Missy, rubbing muck from her eyes, groaned, "That's simply great, Alex. Thanks a lot."

Gabriel's voice came from just outside the craft, "Don't go shootin' us, now! 'Cause we're here to rescue you."

Chapter 13

White Magic

A red-headed teenage girl waded into the wreck and guided Alexandria and Missy out of it. She smiled at the reporters and asked, "Didn't the sheriff and I arrest y'all in Dohiyi?"

Alexandria answered, "I wouldn't mind being locked up again—someplace on solid ground."

Later, in the camp hospital, Missy touched her friend's hand and promised her, "No more choppers. We crossed the whole width of North Carolina—on our feet, or wheels, or hooves—but always close to the ground. No more flying for us."

Ritt spoke from the open doorway: "I promised Miss Keenu to keep y'all out of the combat zone. That means you fly or you stay in camp."

Alexandria complained, "Lieutenant, we already flew—right into your combat zone. Now, Missy has a concussion."

From the bed, Missy argued, "I don't have a concussion. I have a bump."

Ritt frowned and asked Alexandria, "Weren't you supposed to see trouble before it crashed my helo?"

"When my powers become dependable, I'll text you!"

He started to scold her but noticed Jaylan on a cot nearby. He turned toward him and bellowed, "Boy! Who are you and what are you doing in the middle of my war?"

"I'm no one's boy!"

"You're not an adult, and that makes you a boy. What are you doing here?"

"My uncle rescued me from a guarded and comfortable place to drop me in the middle of 'your' war, but my spending the last two years killing zombies makes it my war, too."

Ritt rumbled, "I am Second Lieutenant John Ritt, and you will address me with respect, or you'll be fighting shadows inside the stockade." Cutting off any comeback, he said to Alexandria, "We need your Mama's help, and she wants you out of the battle. So, you go and argue with her about where you and Missy should be." He left without giving the witch's daughter a chance to protest.

Outside, Avianna rested against the railing. Her army-issued black jumpsuit clung to her. She smiled and said, "Lieutenant, those two young women lied to their parents to cross the width of North Carolina through one infected zone after another. Try to confine them, and they'll go off your reservation. I know the type because I am that type."

The narrow walkway forced Ritt to stand close to the seductive vampire. Taking a deep breath, he said, "Keenu doesn't want Alexandria and Missy in the boats."

Avianna purred, "Send the girls to join First Squad. Send Hilanor to protect them. That might reassure the witch." With that, she shrugged and quipped, "Or it might not." Then she turned and walked away.

Approaching from another walk, Keenu stopped two feet from Ritt and asked, "Assure me of what?"

"Your daughter and Missy don't want to fly again. I'm thinking of sending them on the buggies with First Squad and Hilanor."

"I should go with them."

"I need you with the boats."

She sighed and agreed, "Okay, as long as Hilanor goes with them."

That night, Keenu rolled into a fetal position. In her dream, she called her husband.

Martin, who slept in their treehouse village with the black cat, Merlin, dreamt of his wife's calling him. Then found her laying in his arms. "Keenu?" he whispered.

"I'm afraid."

Kissing and stroking her, he whispered, "I love you."

She kissed him, deeply, passionately.

Loving, her heart and soul, he gave her all she needed of him.

When they lay beside each other, breathing hard and spent, she murmured, "Come to the Everglades base and bring Johanna. I need you both."

The next morning, she found the Lieutenant and said, "My husband, Martin, and my daughter, Johanna, are coming. Another tent will be helpful."

"Just like that? No permissions requested?"

"I need them here."

Shaking his head he said, "Of course. What's two more civilians in the middle of all this? I'll make arrangements."

She nodded and headed for the outskirts where the swamp-buggies were being boarded. She called Hilanor to the side and said, "I'm leaving soon with the boats. Missy's in the CSH, so Alexandria will be your primary concern. Keep her safe, Hilanor! You owe me that for your part in Linett's death."

The wizard's once chiseled and handsome face sagged with age. In the humidity, his limp, white hair lost its luster while his eyes remained a penetrating cyan blue. He answered gruffly, "I will do all I can to protect your daughter, without your jabs."

Within the hour, Hilanor and Alexandria boarded the swampbuggy that would take them to join Schwinn and First Squad. They rolled along the trail through the zone Schwinn had already cleared. The four Marines with them dispatched zombies that had wandered back into the area.

One of the Marines groaned, "The more we attract 'em, the more we eradicate 'em, and the more we eradicate 'em, the more our gunfire attracts 'em. It's endless."

"Nope," another counted, "not endless. We started with eight billion people on the planet. Less than half are left. We'll run out of zombies when we run out of people."

The transport caught up to Schwinn's caravan, and Hilanor and Alexandria relocated to the Scout that carried Schwinn and Girl.

He explained to them, "We're clearing areas we haven't seen before on our way southwest to an abandoned visitor's center. Squads from other bases will meet us there. Then, we'll each clear different trails back to our bases. While local authorities are patrolling roads around the 'glades, we'll keep doubling back until we can't find any more biters."

A Marine asked, "Sir, are our boats clearing all the shallow water between here, the Florida Bay, and the Atlantic?"

"We're only responsible for the waterways in the Everglades. Navy Seals, and the Coast Guard are dividing up the rest."

Alexandria strained to understand them through a barrage of visions. As she struggled to separate immediate threats from distant ones, an image—sharp and cold—burst through the pandemonium. She grabbed Sergeant Schwinn's arm and screamed, "Stop the buggies!"

He stopped the caravan, and then shouted, "Why?"

Her honey complexion paled, and tears filled her wide eyes. She swallowed hard before stammering, "W-we'll be ambushed around the next bend! Oh, God, Sergeant! You're going to die."

Without hesitation, he asked, "How many?"

She closed her eyes, probing the vision. "Thirteen," she answered, "One of them is young and scared, but she's armed. There's swamp to the left of the trail and marsh beyond the trees."

Schwinn kept one-third of his people with him to protect Alexandria, Hilanor, and the swampbuggies. He had the white werewolf, Kristian, advance to the right of the pine trees with a group led by DM Marco Coraggio. He had Jamaica advance left of the pines with a group led by the Louisiana sharpshooter, Creole Vanyan.

"The ambushers aren't the only dangers in there," Alexandria whispered to Hilanor.

The wizard climbed down to the ground and pushed the tip of his black staff through pine needles into the sand below. He closed his eyes and intoned,

Nature's creatures, now have fear:
Snakes, 'gators, cats, boar, and bear.
Feel my shifting of this land, and
Leave this space to wolf and man.

Energy from the staff flowed through the ground. A quiver in the land gave the wolves pause. A python slithered away. The gator who had closed in on the Marine's movements, slid back into a nearby pond. A wild hog, foraging for more than his share of vegetation, snorted, and sheltered under a thicket. A golden panther bounded away.

Chapter 14

The Ambusher's Daughter

Corporal Vanyan signaled his detachment and they dropped onto their backs in a head-first position to scull-crawl through the muck under low-hanging branches. The beta wolf, Jamaica, barked for Elderwolf and Girl to follow him on a search for another route.

Reluctant to leave the Marine who had saved her from a python, Girl stalled.

Jamaica growled, and she lowered her head. With a last glance at Witt, she followed the other two wolves.

Vanyan's people inched forward until they cleared the obstructing branches. There, they found the three wolves waiting for them. After a quick body search for the water beetles that could bite into both sides of a finger or toe, Vanyan's group pushed forward.

One of them mumbled to another, "I hate hunting humans! There just aren't enough of us left."

"Better we hunt this bunch than they shoot us."

The three wolves shifted into positions to guard the rear and flanks of Vanyan's group.

***

On the other side of the pines, Corporal Coraggio's detachment—with the alpha wolves, Kristian and Mary—came to a mire. Coraggio and his group low-crawled through the muck. Kristian, having served in the army before becoming a werewolf, plowed in. Mary shook her head twice before following.

The Marines emerged mud-splattered and checked each other for the water beetles while the wolves plucked the insects out of each other's hair.

Then Kristian led them around other obstacles while Mary slipped back to protect their rear. Kristian stopped. He nudged Coraggio, knocking the Marine into a side-step, and growled in the direction of the enemy.

Coraggio radioed his position to Sergeant Schwinn and signaled his people to stay low.

A dingy blue ribbon that was snagged in a shrub caught the wolves' attention. Kristian and Mary sniffed at it then darted ahead. They separated to encircle the hidden ambusher's position.

It turned out to be a trembling girl in ragged overalls. She aimed her rifle toward the sound of oncoming Marines.

From the girl's side, Kristian leapt and clamped his powerful jaws around the rifle barrel. He yanked it out of the hands of the wide-eyed girl and a shot went wild.

Lunging from the other side, Mary knocked the ambusher down, and lay across her thin chest, cutting off her ability to draw a deep breath.

Coraggio emerged from the brush and hissed in the prisoner's ear, "Scream and you die."

Mary shifted to the side, allowing the girl to gasp and then breathe. Another Marine came forward to sit the girl up and bind her tiny wrists.

With the wolves to the right and left of the young prisoner, Coraggio crouched in front of her and asked, "Who are you?"

Grimy and thin, she appeared to be between an adolescent and a young teen. She stared up at one wolf, and then the other. She shivered and tears filled her eyes.

Mary, whose head was larger than the child's, pushed her nose against the girl's cheek. The wolf snarled, exposing her fangs.

The child pleaded, "Please. Pap's out there, and brother, uncles 'n cousins too."

Suppressing thoughts of his wife and child at home, Coraggio grumbled, "You want them to die?"

"No."

"Then, call them. Tell them we're Marines. Now!"

"Pap," she screamed, "Pap! They're Marines. Pap!"

"Tell him he's surrounded."

Shaking her head, she babbled, "We're just a family trying to survive. We need your buggies to get us out-a here. My pap and uncles can't give up."

"Tell them we'll send other vehicles to bring all of you out."

She screamed, "Pap! They'll git us out. Give it up, Pap. Please!"

A sound like a bee zipped over Coraggio's shoulder. He hit the ground as the bullet thudded into the hardwood tree.

The girl ducked and the wolves crouched down.

A salvo shredded the leaves around them.

On the other side of the pine trees, Vanyan heard the girl calling to her people, and then a barrage of gunfire. He shouted into his Comm, "Marco! We'll work our way around them."

Coraggio yelled to Schwinn through the Comm, "Sarge! We're taking fire!"

The Sergeant shouted back to both his Corporals, "Heat 'em up."

Coraggio and Vanyan echoed the command to their detachments, and gunfire shredded the forest.

Birds shrieked and took flight. Small game trembled in the scrub. A family of deer, caught in the crossfire, ran in a circle until Coraggio's people stopped shooting and gave them a way out.

The prisoner wept, "That's my pa in there!"

Coraggio taped her mouth shut, and then he yelled to a white alpha, "Take this kid back to the buggies. Go! Go! Go!"

Mary grabbed the young ambusher's shirt and dragged the kicking and flailing girl backward into the brush.

Kristian wound his way toward the nearest ambusher and gave him no chance to scream or survive.

The Marines shifted from cover to cover, aiming, firing, and hitting each target.

From somewhere in the swamp, a werewolf's cry merged with human screams.

A Marine yelled through the CommLink, "I'm hit!"

A second echoed the first.

A third yelled, "I'm hurt! I can't see!"

"Locations!" Vanyan and Coraggio ordered.

While a corpsman rushed to the blinded Marine's location, Coraggio's and Vanyan's detachments continued to shoot until no one shot back.

The Marines waited and listened: but it was the grunting of zombies that broke the silence.

Chapter 15

Too Long a Werewolf

Coraggio and Vanyan called into their mics, "Get our wounded back to the vehicles!"

Then, the leaders worked their way forward from different directions.

Vanyan stopped short. On the ground ahead of him, the gray wolf and an ambusher lay entangled. Elderwolf had his jaws dug into the man's neck and shoulder. The man had one arm around the wolf, the other between them, and one leg pinned under the wolf's body.

The youngest wolf was there, tearing at the dead man's back.

Vanyan called his coordinates into his CommLink, and said, "I need help over here. And send Jamaica: fast!"

Other Marines arrived and one asked, "You want us in the middle of this, Corporal?"

"Help me untangle 'em." Vanyan ordered, "Careful with the gray. I think he's wounded."

Pointing at the young wolf, another Marine quipped, "I'm more worried about her!"

Baring her fangs, Girl snapped at the Marines who came close.

Dripping blood from his snout and black hair, Jamaica appeared like a fiend in a nightmare. He nipped at Girl's flank and she snarled but backed away.

The Marines separated the two entwined forms, revealing Elderwolf's bleeding flank, and a revolver in the ambusher's cold grip.

Four Marines helped the gray wolf to his feet then backed away.

The wolf fell again then struggled to stand.

Girl and Jamaica went to his side.

Vanyan said, "I can hear Zombies coming. We need to reach the swampbuggies."

With Jamaica and Girl on each side of him, the oldest wolf limped toward the trail.

Vanyan ordered one Marine, "Go with 'em." To the others he said, "We still have wounded out there."

Just as Vanyan spoke, Coraggio called coordinates and said, "I need help here!"

Girl sniffed the air and froze. Then she spun away from Jamaica and Elderwolf and ran full-speed toward Witt's scent.

As she burst from cover, Coraggio and two other Marines stepped back from their fallen comrade.

The young wolf sniffed at the bullet wound on Witt's side and whined. Then she sniffed at the bullet wound in his head, raised herself on her hind legs, and released a prolonged and agonized howl that chilled the seasoned warriors around her.

After her second howl, Coraggio said, "Girl! Zombies are coming. We need to carry Witt out of here."

Ears back and fangs dripping saliva, the young wolf held her ground.

"Girl, you know we have to get him back to the buggies."

The stench of zombies and the buzz of flies told the wolf that the Corporal was right. Raising her ears, she let Witt's comrades carry him.

At the swampbuggies, Alexandria waited with Hilanor and Sergeant Schwinn. A noise drew their attention to the tree line where a white wolf emerged, dragging a struggling child onto the trail.

Alexandria said, "In my visions, that kid was with the ambushers."

Schwinn directed a Marine to put the weeping child on his Scout and guard her.

Then, Alexandria grabbed Schwinn's arm saying, "Sergeant! Mary's hurt—shot!"

With visible effort, Mary leapt onto the bed of the Sportsman and a second corpsman rushed over to help her. He pulled an anesthetic from his bag but, when he brought the needle near the wolf, she snarled at him. He put the needle away. Taking a ragged breath, he began removing the bullet without anesthesia.

Mary lay still and allowed the corpsman to help her. She only moved her head when she scented the arrival of Elderwolf and Jamaica.

Jamaica lay under the Sportsman while Elderwolf leapt onto the swampbuggy and dropped near Mary.

The corpsman paled at the sight of a second wounded wolf filling the narrow walkway.

Kristian emerged from the tree line and laid under the Sportsman near his beta.

Alexandria climbed down from the Scout and walked over to the Sportsman. She brought out her camera and took photos of the wounded wolves. When Kristian raised his head and stared at her, she said, "People need to know what you've risked for us." Unwilling to push her luck, she returned to the Scout.

The smell of decay and the sounds of shuffling and grunting reached Mary. Unable to rise with her side opened, she growled. Elderwolf struggled to his feet and howled.

Six zombies emerged from the trees.

The Marines opened fire.

Schwinn grabbed the wizard's arm and half-helped, half-hoisted him into the Scout, just before turning to shoot a zombie who closed in on him.

Alexandria wrapped her arms around the still muffled and bound child who struggled against her. The older girl snapped, "I'm trying to shield you."

The girl babbled through the gag. When Alexandria removed it, the child shouted, "Give me a fuckin' gun!"

"I don't have one."

"Who comes into the 'glades withouten a gun?"

Alexandria snapped, "Me—with my own squad of Marines!"

From the Scout, Schwinn kept firing. As Marines emerged from the brush, firing at zombies behind them, the Sergeant called for air support.

Girl arrived with Coraggio, who carried Witt's body over his shoulder, and other Marines helping wounded comrades. Coraggio eased Witt's body onto the Sportsman, and Girl leapt onboard. The other two wounded Marines were helped into seats.

The corpsman, stitching Mary, but surrounded by more wounded, yelled, "I need help here! Anybody with hands! Anybody! Now!"

The Marines who brought the wounded jumped on board.

Kristian and Jamaica scrambled out from under the Scout and boarded the less crowded Explorer.

A medivac flew over them.

On Schwinn's order, the Sportsman continued down the trail, taking the wounded Marines and Witt's body to wait for the medevac. He ordered the other men, "Contain the zombies and light up the forest." Then he radioed for a helitanker.

As soon as the woodland ignited, the fire spread. Hissing, spitting, and roaring flames consumed pine trees, shrubs, dead ambushers, and the zombies that never screamed. Plumes of smoke mushroomed, and they unfurled, carrying a toxic mix of burning organics. As the inferno flashed and crackled in the treetops, the Marines stopped to monitor the breezes that threatened to blow the flames their way.

In the Scout, Alexandria sat near the prisoner who cried, "You see'in this? That's my family you're burnin' up in there! Pap, Brother, my uncles and cousins. You're killin' all of 'em! Gone!"

Alexandria said, "I'm sorry, but they shot first."

"Afterin' you took me! Y'all did that first!"

Lying on the walkway, Kristian and Jamaica glared at the child that carried the enemy's scents

The Marines who had disembarked with Schwinn formed brigades. Using the water from their supplies, they created a short, muddy demarcation line. As the fire threatened to leap it, the welcome sound of the helitankers eased their fears, but Schwinn yelled, "Under the buggies, now!"

Half a dozen different aircraft, each with the marking of a different fire department, dropped water on the fire. Schwinn recognized a Bell with red stripes on the propellers and a Firehawk with blue stripes. He identified one more as a red, fixed-wing craft. The other three he did not know.

The water cascaded over the flames, and the trees that were not yet burning. He smiled with gratitude for the pilots who had survived the zombie infection.

After the tankers reduced the blaze to cinders, the Marines, wearing gas masks because of the acrid smoke, raised tents for a temporary encampment.

The wounded wolves rested in a makeshift hospital. Unable to wear the masks. Mary and Elderwolf, struggled with the smoke, but still healed faster than the humans would.

Chapter 16

Feral Descent

Inside the hospital tent, the staff ran ventilation equipment to keep the air as clean as possible for the injured wolves. Elderwolf whined in his sleep.

In the tent next to it, Girl lay beside Witt's stretcher. Her hazel eyes narrowed, and she snarled with each breath. Four Marines entered—but the wolf growled at them and they froze. The Marine who owned two large Newfoundlands eased forward. Hoping the human within the wolf still understood him, he said, "Girl, we need to send Witt home. A helo came to take him back to base. Then they'll fly him to Arlington Cemetery."

Girl snarled.

Unabated, the Marine explained, "Witt's a hero, Girl. The people who transport our dead honor them." He strengthened his voice to add, "Leaving Witt here does not honor him."

Head down, she bared her fangs.

The young Marine whispered to another, "Get one of them white wolves."

When Kristian padded into the tent with Jamaica following, the three huge wolves filled the floor space. The humans backed against the canvas walls.

Kristian approached Girl.

Saliva dripped from her fangs. She clamped her jaws around the leg of the stretcher and snorted.

Ears back, Kristian barked a warning. When she did not release the stretcher, he lunged at her. He bit through the outer hair on the side of her throat and into the fur next to the skin. He yanked her head sideways, pulling the stretcher off balance.

Girl released and snapped at her alpha.

Jamaica howled, letting Mary and Elderwolf know about trouble. Their cries rose and fell in a pitch that chilled every human in camp.

When the Marines shifted to grab the stretcher, Girl lunged at the closest one.

Kristian grabbed her by the back of her neck and rolled her onto her side, crashing an end table and chair to the ground. He straddled her and bit into the hair under her chin.

She twisted her body, clawing at his belly; then she bit deep into his side.

The white werewolf yelped in pain and clamped down harder on the back of Girl's neck. He twisted until young brown wolf yelped. He backed off, staying close enough for another attack.

Jamaica's human loyalty kept him from joining Girl's challenge of their Alpha.

Wet, and ragged around Kristian's bites, Girl stood. With her head hanging and her tail between her legs, she trembled.

The alpha raised his head and tail to signal the end of the fight. He knew what he could not say: that Girl should not remain a wolf much longer. He left the tent, with Jamaica following, and Girl trailing.

The golden-brown wolf did not look back at the stretcher. Outside, she stopped to sniff the air. A lingering cloud of smoke made sorting the different scents difficult. Still, she recognized the Marines' combinations of cotton camo, boots, weapons, and food rations. She also recognized the smell of the herbs and incense the wizard and young witch carried. Only one person in camp carried the same scent as the people who killed Witt.

Girl stopped trailing Kristian and Jamaica. Following the scent of the young ambusher, she found the right tent and lay down alongside it, waiting.

Inside Alexandria and Hilanor sat on side-by-side cots eating MREs. They used the flameless heater included in each packet. Alexandria frowned, while Hilanor wrinkled his nose.

Bound, but not gagged, the ambusher lay on a third cot. Curled under a thin blanket with her back to them. She had refused food and alternated between silence and sniffles.

The tent flap rustled and someone entered, startling Alexandria. The witch's daughter recovered and leapt to hug her tall, slim, blonde best friend. She laughed and said, "Missy! What are you doing here? You have a concussion."

"I hitch-hiked on the medivac. We've survived everything before this—together. We're not separating now."

Alexandria said to the old wizard, "You never met Missy. I had an aunt that would say, 'Bless her heart, here she is.'"

"Keenu speaks highly of you, young lady—despite her anger that the two of you crossed North Carolina—alone—to reach the battle in Dohiyi."

Missy grinned and answered, "Believe me; my parents had burrs under their saddles for months." She sat next to Alexandria and asked, "What're you eating? I'm starving."

Alexandria handed her the remainder of her MRE, saying, "It's not home cooking."

Between bites, Missy said, "Fill me in. Did you take photos?"

"You ladies catch up," Hilanor suggested, "while I find another cot."

Turning back to her friend, Alexandria answered, "Yes, photos and notes. You?"

"I've been writing about life in the main camp. Now that we're together, we can combine what we have and send reports to our bloggers."

Alexandria sighed and said, "I'm so glad you're here. I feel responsible for the injuries and a death today. I kept being hit by too many images—too fast—to sort them all." Tears filled her eyes as she reached out and held her friend's hand.

"The injuries, the death: they're not on you! Sweet Lord, Alexandria! Shit's happening all the time, everywhere. We're damn lucky when you can warn us!"

Alexandria shook her head.

Missy put her arm around her friend, suggesting, "Maybe, when you can't see it or sort it out, it's because that future keeps changing. All I know is that I wouldn't have reached Dohiyi alive if you hadn't been able to see the danger around each corner." She let go of Alexandria to resume eating the cold and dry chicken. After taking more bites, she tilted her head toward the child, and asked, "Who's that?"

"Suzette," the girl snapped. Twisting to face them, she added, "I'm Suzette—and, if y'all think your scarin' me wit all that mumbo jumbo, forgit it. My Mam's family is Louisiani, so I know all about witchy stuff." With that, she twisted back toward the tent wall.

Missy laughed, "There's a tough boy in camp who's either going to love or hate this one."

The tent flap rustled again, and Schwinn entered with two guards. He announced, "The child is going back to base, now. The rest of us will break camp in the morning to go on to our meeting at the next visitor's center."

The eleven-year-old faced the wall but protested, "I ain't goin' no-wheres."

"You'll walk or be carried."

Not wanting further humiliation, Suzette struggled to stand with her wrists still bound. Despite being accustomed to the heat, she perspired.

Girl, slinking behind tents and shrubs, followed the ambusher's daughter to a revving helicopter. As the helicopter rose, tilted, and flew away, Girl followed below. She stayed out of sight until she made it to the trail beyond camp. Then she burst into full speed. She would not be able to catch up to the helo, but she would be able to keep it in sight.

In the hospital tent, Mary sniffed the air for the rest of the pack. Finding only a faint scent for Girl, she struggled to her feet and howled for the others. With effort, Elderwolf raised himself and joined her call. Outside, Kristian and Jamaica stood and howled in unison.

Schwinn ran up and yelled, "What in Hell is going on, now?" He glanced around and asked, "Where's Girl?" A heartbeat later, he grumbled, "Damn! Has she really gone after Witt?" He turned to Kristian and said, "I need the rest of you. Can you send only one after her?"

With that, Jamaica bolted for the trail.

Schwinn radioed Ritt and said: "Lieutenant, you have trouble coming your way."

Chapter 17

Stalker

The helicopter landed in Ritt's camp, and the dignified Carry Team brought Witt's body to the makeshift morgue. Corpsmen helped injured Marines to the field hospital, while guards brought Suzette to the Lieutenant for additional questioning: during which she remained belligerent.

Inside the hospital's, thirty-by-thirty patient, room, Jaylan—whose minor wounds had healed—helped the new patients settle into their cots. He held a glass for a burn patient and kept covered a blinded one. The different squads in camp had served together in Dohiyi and strengthened their bond through every campaign since. One of them had a photo near his bed of himself smiling with Witt.

Nearby, Shea ignored her food tray. The bite from a brown recluse spider still ate the flesh of her hand, and the appendage had swollen to twice its normal size. Jaylan steadied her tray and coaxed her into eating.

As the guards nudged Suzette inside the hospital, Marines wounded by her family scowled.

Ignoring their glares, she retained her hardened expression. Then she lay on her cot and stared at the ceiling. Her eyes had reddened from crying and smoke, and mud still streaked and knotted her brown hair.

A wiry guard, older than the others, handcuffed her to the cot.

She scowled first at him and then at the boy helping a wounded teenager across the room. "Why's that black one free?" she demanded to know.

"Because he's on our side."

"Then ah guess I'll be hatin' him forever, too!"

"Suit yourself, kiddo."

She watched the boy help the teenager. The girl had a wealth of red curls and jade green eyes. Suzette whispered to herself, "I'll be that pretty someday" –but the thought that followed was, probably not.

A corpsman pulled the curtain around Suzette to examine her. He made notes about her dehydration and malnourishment. He also made note of the bruises and lacerations common to jungle fighting. He found no signs of abuse and, even more important, no wolf bites.

An hour later, a cart came from the galley with hot food and Jaylan helped distribute the meals.

As he approached Suzette, she snapped a slur and rolled away from him.

The boy grumbled, "Asshole. You shot at these guys. You think I'll cry if you starve to death?"

The doctors gaped at the boy, but the Marines nodded.

"I don't want your tears or your germs."

"This or nothing—and, please, choose nothing."

She buried her face in the pillow.

Jaylan turned away. The room filled with wounded reminded the boy that his uncle's death would leave him alone again. Veins in his temples throbbed and his stomach churned. Still, he kept helping.

Outside, at the end of a walkway, Avianna enjoyed her view of the constellations above and the aromas of the flowers around her. When a different scent caught her attention, she turned toward the marsh and said, "Ah, Girl, I smell your human blood within the wolf. I hear your beating heart. Who do you stalk, *piccolo lupo*? Oh, but it is the ambusher's child, is it not? Now, your pulse has quickened." Avianna stayed quiet for a second before adding, "I have one caution for you. I, who understand vengeance, have never killed a child. Such a killing may end the remnants of your humanity." When the creature's breathing did not change, the vampire said, "Oh well. Unless you hunt me or mine, your business is not my business." With that, Avianna walked away, giving the young wolf no more thought.

Not interested in the vampire, Girl resumed her hunt for Suzette. Maneuvering through the brush and onto solid land, she followed the child's scent to the field hospital. There the golden-brown wolf leaned back on her haunches then sprung at the door slamming it open.

Suzette saw her and screamed. Wounded and medicated soldiers sat upright, unable to stand. Jaylan scrambled from his cot. Hauling his backpack with him, he jumped on Suzette's cot and yelled, "Behind me! Stay behind me." He pulled his gun from his backpack and took aim.

Confused by the boy's having Jamaica's scent, Girl focused on the one who cowered behind him. Her head dropped between her shoulders and her saliva dripped onto the planked floor.

Shea, rushing to stand in front of Jaylan, shouted, "That's Girl! She should know me."

Suzette cried from behind them, "Are-ya nuts? Kill it! Kill it!"

Shea yelled at the wolf, "What the hell's wrong with you, Girl? Have you forgotten what side you're on?" Shea softened her tone. "Listen, Girl," she said, "You and me—we're about the same age. Instead of going to proms, we kill zombies and lose people we love, but we must still do what's right."

The werewolf angled to go around Shea and Jaylan.

Shea's pulse jumped and her voice quickened, "Jesus, can't you still think at all? Remember who you are! This boy's Jamaica's son. Girl! Stop!"

Girl wavered. She had trouble understanding the words, but she knew the name, Jamaica, and smelled his scent in the boy.

Behind Girl, a Marine slid off his bunk and dragged himself to a side table from which he grabbed a pair of scissors. Clutching the almost useless weapon, he dragged himself toward the large werewolf.

Girl's golden eyes blazed with unnatural light.

Behind Shea, Jaylan whispered, "Move Shea! I can take care of myself." Behind him, Suzette sobbed.

Girl crouched for a lunge.

Jamaica crashed through the door and body-slammed the young wolf to the floor.

Suzette, seeing the larger wolf, screamed.

Shea, remembering him from Dohiyi, breathed the name, "Jamaica."

Jaylan, confused by hearing his father's name, lowered his gun, while Suzette fainted.

Jamaica and Girl nipped and bit the back of each other's necks. The black wolf had the advantage of size. The golden-brown wolf had the advantage of hate. Everyone else backed against the walls as the fighting wolves knocked over tables and empty cots.

Snarls mixed with wails. Girl crouched and yelped with her tail between her legs then attacked again. Jamaica took the smaller wolf to her back, biting under her neck and her abdomen. Girl rolled to her side to snap at Jamaica's legs and claw her way back onto her feet.

Two Marines burst into the hospital with Keenu and Avianna behind them.

One of the Marines aimed his rifle at Girl, and Avianna tore it from his hands saying, "*No. Non Ancora*—not yet!"

Keenu pushed her way to the front and, seeing the result of her curse, lifted her hand. Above the commotion, she shouted,

God of sun, God of moon,
God of wolf, God of man,
For this girl in hatred's maw,
Break the bind of hand to claw.
Let her see the moon's true face.
Return her to her human grace.

The room went silent as Girl thrashed in agony. Only the Marines from Dohiyi had seen a werewolf in transition. Every other human gasped as Girl's hocks cracked and bent in their opposite directions. Her long hair and the thick fur beneath drew back into the werewolf's body.

Avianna yanked a blanket from the nearest cot and covered the mutating wolf.

After Girl's immeasurable anguish, her human shape lay naked and shivering under the blanket. Only her light brown pixie-cut hair and the face of a waif lie uncovered.

Avianna ordered the doctors and staff, "*Aiutala! Adesso!*" When they did not act, she translated, "*Idiote!* Help her: now!"

Corpsmen rushed forward and carried Girl to a cot. They pulled a privacy curtain around her and began dressing the deepest bites on her body. Another corpsman checked on Suzette.

Avianna said to Keenu, "Fast thinking."

Keenu grunted, "I wrote the reverse when I wrote the spell but, right now, we need to leave the doctors to their work."

"Wait!" Jaylan yelled, "Don't nobody leave until Shea tells me why she called that—" he pointed to the black wolf, "—Jamaica."

The vampire rolled her eyes. "Ah," she said, "this tangled web is not mine." Then, she turned and left.

Pale and trembling, Shea said, "Sorry Jaylan. I only know that the Marines in Dohiyi called the black werewolf Jamaica, and that I need to lie down." She dragged herself back to her bunk and slid under the thin cover. She draped her arm over her eyes and ignored everything except her fatigue and the pulsing, burning pain in her hand.

Jaylan turned to Keenu and asked, "Are you the witch that sent the water funnel to save my uncle and me?"

"Yes."

"Why does this wolf have my father's name?"

Jamaica tucked his tail under his rump. Ears twitching, he hung his head. He came as close to looking sheepish as possible for a huge wolf.

"Okay," Keenu said, "You two, Jamaica and Jaylan, come with me."

The wolf slunk behind his son and the witch.

Keenu led them to the outermost walkway where she composed herself before telling the werewolf, "You didn't tell him, so now I have too! I'm not happy."

Jaylan yelled, "You told him to tell me what? What the fuck?"

A gust of hot wind ruffled their clothing and hair. The surface of the water rippled below the walkway. Keenu calmed herself, and the wind subsided. "Now listen to me, Jaylan Savann," she instructed, "I don't care how you talked on the street, or in your gang, or in the orphanage. I do not allow my girls to use that language with me, and I will not have you aiming trash at me either."

"You're not my mother!"

A powerful wind swirled around the boy and lifted him off his feet. An owl screeched nearby. The witch grumbled, "I'm not your mama. I'm Keenu Kulae, and I will be respected—or your feet won't touch the ground until your next birthday."

Jamaica growled at the witch.

Fists clenched Jaylan grumbled, "I'm sorry!" Then he muttered, "Shit" —and rushed to repeat, "Sorry."

Keenu scowled and said, "Because your papa never told me any of this, I can only repeat what I've heard. Years before the zombie infection, he drove a cab in Cincinnati. One night he picked up a fare: a werewolf in human form. She bit him." Keenu took a breath. Then, she continued, "I don't know what happened when he was a wolf, but the story goes that, when he became human again, he was terrified he might hurt you and your mama. So, he ran. Mary and Kristian found him, and he did what wolves do; he stayed with his adopted pack."

Jaylan remembered his mother's turning into a zombie, and the explosion of gunfire when he shot her. The shell-shocked boy glared at the massive black wolf and yelled, "You're huge and strong, but didn't come back to save Mom! You didn't come back to save me either!" Shivering in the Florida heat, he cried, "You're a coward. You're such a coward that you sent my uncle to get me!"

The witch took the boy by the shoulders. Softening her voice, she explained, "There's no uncle. The orphanage had a record of your father being dead, so he said he was his brother." She released him and moved aside.

The boy sputtered, "N-no uncle? You're a liar, too?"

The wolf looked away.

Jaylan screamed, "I need you human! Now!"

"He can't," Keenu explained, "because I put the werewolves under a spell to remain wolves. I only made Girl human again because she became feral."

Shaking his head, the boy said, "I don't give a shit about your curse, or this battle, or zombies. Nothing will ever be worse for me than this."

"I'm truly sorry, Jaylan, but they need to stay wolves. Try to believe that he cares."

Jaylan moaned, "It doesn't matter if that's true. It's not enough." He spun around and ran back to the hospital.

Jamaica turned to follow him, but Keenu said, "No. Alexandria called before all this happened. With Elderwolf and Mary shot, and Girl transformed, Schwinn's squad needs you. But, for that boy's sake, don't die."

The werewolf whined and leapt over a railing. He plowed through the marsh then disappeared into the trees.

Chapter 18

The Gathering

Blending with the night, Jamaica slipped into Schwinn's encampment and found Kristian under the Explorer. The white wolf raised his head to acknowledge his beta, and then he lowered his head and closed his eyes. Jamaica scratched away pine needles and nestled into the sand next to his alpha. The bites from his fight with Girl had already healed.

In the swampbuggy above him, Mary's bullet wound had healed enough for her to breathe easy and sleep, but Elderwolf shuddered and whined through the night.

Morning came and the squad pushed forward through the burned swamp. Smoke painted the sky orange, and a lingering haze obstructed their view. Floating particles from the ashen plants and peat moss stung their eyes, scratched their throats, and gave them headaches. The wolves' had a harder time breathing the sooty air than the humans.

Kristian decided that the caravan's pace, and the Marines stopping often to clear the trail, risked his pack. He howled for the other wolves to follow him, and they all leaped from the buggies and ran.

A human exercising can breathe forty to sixty times a minute, but the wolves—at full run—breathed up to three-hundred-and-fifty times a minute. They would clear the fire zone sooner but inhale more toxins.

The wolves crossed the charred terrain as fast as Elderwolf could travel and soon outdistanced the squad. From his seat in the buggy, Schwinn watched them leave and trusted them to wait for him in a cleared zone. He coughed up phlegm. Then he planned his next report. He ordered a Private to take photos of the fire damage and the corpses. They would become evidence that Marines and firefighters had controlled the spread of the fire, and that the squad had made a dent in the local zombie population. Photos of young sprouts poking through surviving patches of peat were evidence of forest regeneration. That might pacify those environmentalists who cared more about trees than zombied humans.

Kristian's pack emerged from the burned zone onto green grass. In a nearby channel, a congregation of alligators closed in, but their keen sense of smell warned them away from the unnatural beings. As the alligators retreated, the wolves drank from the clearest threads of water. To escape the smoke that a strong breeze carried toward them, Jamaica and Kristian dug tunnels where Mary and Elderwolf could rest; then they dug shallower ones from which they would monitor the alligators watching them from the far embankment.

Just before nightfall, the swampbuggies emerged from the burned zone into the open field. Not having seen an ambulatory zombie since before the fire, Schwinn ordered the buggies to stop and his Marines to make camp. He turned to his Corporals, Coraggio and Vanyan, and said, "According to my last communication with Lieutenant Ritt, the squads that cleared the way from the west and northwest are waiting for us at an abandoned visitors center. We should reach them early tomorrow."

Coraggio glanced at the werewolves who emerged from their tunnels, and said, "The white female looks recovered, but the older one's not looking great."

Vanyan nodded in Mary's direction, "What ah wouldn't give to heal like that!"

Coraggio grinned and replied, "I don't think you'd give all they gave."

Gumbo-limbo tree branches sagged under the collective weight of birds that had fled the fire. Their songs brought other birds, and their movements dislodged fruit that dropped to the small creatures on the ground.

Coraggio laughed, "If I could have a superpower, I'd choose flight."

As the Marines settled in for the night, the wolves closed their eyes but stayed alert. The next day, Schwinn's squad and the wolf pack reached the gathering place without new incidents.

A second-story roofed bridge connected two large pink buildings. Long neglected, the buildings needed paint. An oval garden in front of the main entrance was overgrown. The beautiful lawns pictured in brochures had yielded to sand and scrub.

To the sides of the buildings, a couple dozen civilians ate and talked in small groups. Marine tents formed a protective barrier around them.

A Private greeted Sergeant Schwinn and led him to a meeting room where commanding officers from the other squads talked with civilian leaders. After introductions, the Sergeant took a seat.

The already cantankerous discussion focused on the civilian need to defend themselves and their homes, while the military cleared zombie herds from areas like the 'glades.

A man in a worn business suit raised his voice and said, "The American population is about forty percent what it was before the infection. Police, firefighters, and the military have all lost more. What can you still do?"

Schwinn answered, "We have been, are, and will keep doing all we can, but civilians need to help each other—or the infection will keep spreading."

A young man said, "It's not my job to mess with them biters."

A young woman in clean white shorts and a tank-top yelled, "I'm not a cop or soldier. My husband can't handle a gun. It's your job and the police's job to protect our homes and families!"

Schwinn snapped, "Then you'll die because we can't be everywhere. If you call the police to get a zombie out of your house, you will be bitten before they can arrive."

"It's not fair," she cried.

Another commander answered, "No. It's not fair, but I'm guessing every soldier who lost family was defending someone else at the time. My sister's dead because I was with my unit. That's our new reality."

Schwinn raised a hand and offered, "If you want to learn to protect yourselves, my people can give some gun-safety lessons after the meeting."

One of four grizzled old men in the back of the room raised his hand and added, "An' those of us who live in the glades can help give lessons to them suburbees. I been shooting 'gaters since I was eight-year-old."

Another woman, middle-aged with dark circles under her eyes cut him off, and argued, "Thou shalt not kill! I will not kill anyone, not even those poor retched creatures. I have stayed alive by hiding and I will keep hiding!"

The old man snapped back: "An' you can only keep hidin' 'cause other people are doin' the killin' for you? You think them zombies let your food delivery through out of the kindness of their rotted hearts?"

While the arguing continued inside, Alexandria took photos of the camp, and Missy made notes. Bloggers continued to trust the accuracy of the young reporters' transmissions, and the girls were determined to continue earning that trust. When they finished gathering information, they found their way around the buildings to where the wolves rested on a raised, sun-soaked platform overlooking a glistening lake. Alexandria sat next to Jamaica, and Missy sat on Alexandria's left.

Alexandria extended her hand to stroke the black wolf.

Head down, ears back, Jamaica snarled.

Red-faced, Alexandria yanked back her hand and said, "Sorry. I'm sorry.

Missy gaped and whispered to her friend, "They're not pets."

Alexandria whispered back, "I wasn't thinking."

Missy changed the subject by raising her voice and asking, "Where's the light brown wolf: Girl?"

Alexandria blanched and shuddered. Eyes squeezed shut, she rubbed her forehead with a shaking hand.

Missy touched her friend's shoulder and asked, "What? What do you see?"

The witch's daughter kept her eyes closed. Despite the Florida heat, she shivered as she answered, "I think I'm seeing the past. Girl's in the CSH, fighting with . . ." She cut off, not wanting to identify Jamaica. She opened her eyes and continued, "She was after Suzette. My mama broke the spell and made Girl human again." To wolves who were staring at her, she repeated, "Girl's human again!"

She turned toward Missy and cried, "Dark magic's very dangerous—and, without her coven to anchor her, Mama could lose herself in it."

Missy asked, "I don't understand that."

"Subverting a human's free-will or changing a physical body—that takes dark magic." Touching Missy's hand, Alexandria murmured, "Dark magic is addictive and soul-altering. The more a witch uses it the more likely she is to be overtaken by it—and my mother's done it at least twice before this. Missy, she has to stop before she gets lost in it."

The white werewolf, Mary, growled.

Alexandria responded, "I'm sorry. I saw Girl morph into a human, but nothing else came through."

A Private approached and interrupted them: "We've set up tents for y'all tonight. Come this way."

As they followed him, Alexandria moved into position next to Jamaica and said, "I know Jaylan's your son, and I saw him stand between the young werewolf and Suzette. Even terrified, he was brave. I also saw your fight with Girl and know you had to do it." Alexandria's fingertips touched his hair. This time, he stood still.

Missy and Alexandria entered their tent and sat side-by-side on a cot. Missy said to her friend, "I'm worried that your visions might mess with your head."

"We're in a zombie war fought by witches, werewolves, vampires—and Marines and human ambushers, too. Trust me, my head's already a mess."

"Well, I saw you stroking that werewolf. Please, Alex, remember that—in human form—he's too old for you. He's already a father, but we're still in college. And you barely know him."

"I know him better than you think. I've been having visions about him. I've seen how brave he was in Dohiyi; his being that magnificent black wolf running through zombie-clogged alleys to carry saddlebags of ammunition to the Marines and militia fighters. His dangerous trip north to find his son—and then not able to say he's Jaylan's dad because Jaylan's dad's supposed to be dead." Tears flowed as she struggled to add, "I saw him bitten and turned and abandoning his family to save them—from him! Missy, I know this man. And with half the people in the world gone, age doesn't matter to me anymore."

"I-I didn't know."

"I'm so tired."

The pretty blonde stood and said, "Then sleep, now." When Alexandria laid down, Missy covered her and moved to the other cot.

Missy lay down, but sleep would not come. Smoke damage was bad enough, but a new question jolted her: Keenu. What kind of damage would Keenu do if she and her magic became permanently dark? Missy tried to clear her mind, but her new worry festered.

Chapter 19

Demons and Disciples

The next evening, Schwinn's filthy and insect-bitten squad drove back to the main camp. Despite exhaustion, they stopped to clean their weapons before hitting the showers. In the showers, a man teased Kowolski, "Hey, K-o-w-o-l-s-k-i, were y'all too backwoods to spell it K-o-w-a-l-s-k-i?"

"Man, we were just too Ellis Island. The guy at a desk wrote it, and mama kept the spelling thinking it was American." After the showers, Kowolski and the others went to the galley where they spread out among the people already there.

In the hospital, Avianna ran a donation through the blood warmer while Joseph stood nearby with the cow's blood the cooks in the galley had given him. The stench of infection tainted the scent of the humans around them.

Patients and staff pretended not to see Avianna pour warmed blood into her crystal goblet.

One of the Marines playing cards with Shea tilted his head toward the door through which the vampires had left and sighed, "We're supposed to feel safer in camp, but I don't feel safer. Do you?"

"My meemaw would say, 'Sweetheart, you're the shackled Goat in Jurassic Park.'" Shea's spider-bitten hand refused to heal, so her poker partners helped her fan and discard her cards.

As the doctors made their rounds, two of them stopped at the bed of the comatose young werewolf. One said, "We're gambling that medically induced sleep will give this kid time to readjust to being human, but how long do we keep her under?"

Shaking his head, the other one answered, "No idea. We just don't want her waking up homicidal."

From his cot, Jaylan scowled at Girl. His eyes closed, and her wolf sprang from the shadows. Her hazel eyes changed to black. Jamaica, with drooling white fangs, snarled and snapped at him.

Jaylan jolted upright. He glanced around and took a deep breath. He missed his mother even more than he had before he knew his dad lived but trusted no one enough to share that hurt.

A corpsman came over and asked, "Jay, are you hungry?"

"No, thank you."

After the corpsman left, Shea broke from her poker game and sat on the edge of the boy's cot. She fumbled with her thick, red hair unable to knot it with only one unbandaged hand. "I lived in Dohiyi," she said, "and fought in its militia. I might be able to answer a question or two about your daddy."

Jaylan shook his head.

"Well, whether you want to know or not, your pa and Girl wore saddlebags and carried a crazy amount of heavy ammunition from supply to our positions. Without them, and the other wolves who did the same, we would have had to send our people through those zombie mobs. That girl," she pointed to the unconscious werewolf, "and your daddy saved a lot of us."

"He didn't save my mother and he left me on the streets."

"Listen Jaylan, Schwinn's group has had a rough time. They've had Marines and wolves wounded and one Marine is dead. Your daddy's risking his life to help them."

"He's risking his life for his food supply—like all the supernaturals."

"His pack doesn't hunt humans."

"Says who? Them?"

"You're a stubborn little mule, aren't you?

Jaylan did not hear her over the crack of his gunfire when he shot his mother. His zombied mom had collapsed in a pool of her own blood while his wolfed-out father saved strangers. A tear slid sideways into his hair.

Shea sighed and said, "Okay, I only have one more thing to say: the zombies got my daddy and mama. Then, while I fought alongside the militia, my sister showed up on the battlefield already bitten. The way you shot your mama, I shot my younger sister—but I only had to shoot her because I hadn't stayed home to protect her. Jaylan, you're lucky to still have a daddy if you want him." She went back to her poker game.

On the cot next to Jaylan's, the ten-year-old prisoner, Suzette, rolled toward him. Pale and trembling, she hissed, "Well, I ain't got no Pap. Not 'cause of zombies. 'Cause of your animal army."

He waved at the wounded and said, "You call these Marines animals, again, and I'll bust your face. Your thieving family shot at them when they were only there to clear out zombies."

"You fools kill't and burnt all I had left of my kin. God's witness! I don't got nothin' left to bury an' nowhere left to live." She rolled away from him and closed her eyes. A kaleidoscope of images filled her mind: the Marines murdering her family, the unconscious girl growing right out of a wolf, and the ghost-like woman with the long hair, pouring blood into a fancy glass. Fear clanged like a hammer against the inside of her head. What if everyone there came out of an animal? What if the food she'd been given changed her into a beast? Waves of despair washed through the child, and she buried her face in her pillow.

Schwinn strode into the hospital with Alexandria and Jamaica behind him. The Sergeant said to the doctors, "Make sure you keep Girl sedated. We need to keep our prisoner safe."

The wolf and the witch's daughter approached Jaylan.

Staying on his back, the boy scowled at his father and said, "No! I can't talk to you when you're like that."

"You don't have to talk to him. Just accept him; that's all he wants."

"Yeah? How do you know what he wants?" Jaylan sat upright to be eye-level with the huge werewolf, "Go away. Come back when you only have two legs."

The black wolf narrowed his eyes, lay his ears back, and snarled.

"He's your papa," Alexandria said.

Jaylan did not respond.

Sergeant Schwinn worked his way around the room, talking to each of his wounded Marines until he reached Jaylan's cot. With the wolf and Alexandria on one side, the Sergeant went to the space between Jaylan's cot and Suzette's. Gruff and frowning, he said, "Jaylan, we need the wolves to stay wolves to scout for us—even if that's a problem for you."

Jaylan lay back down. Focusing on the ceiling, he said, "Fine, but I don't have to talk to him when he looks like that."

Alexandria sighed and said, "Well, my family's waiting for me in the galley. I'll see y'all later."

As Alexandria left, a corpsman came to treat Suzette's wounds. With the Sergeant between the beds, the corpsman went to the other side. He unbound the ten-year-old and began changing the bandages on the deepest scratches she'd received while being dragged out of the woods. The child closed her eyes trying to remember the last thing her father said to her. His voice came through her memories: "We gotta be our own avenging angels, Suzette, 'cause God's given up on this world." The child's eyes opened and wandered to the attendant's tray. She was relieved to see medicines, gauze, tape, and scissors instead of food that might turn her into an animal.

Standing between the children's cots, Schwinn said to Jaylan, "Listen, we were all fighting to save Dohiyi instead of saving our own families. And we're here, doing it again, leaving the safety of our families to local police. That's what the military does, and that's what your father did."

Behind the sergeant, Suzette thought about all the people who encouraged the boy to accept an animal as his father. There were so many of them: the red head they called Shea, the heavy woman they called Alexandria, and the Marine with his back to her who had led the ones who killed her family. The child thought, 'This surely must be Hell.'

A patient convulsed and fell from his cot. The corpsman treating Suzette ran to help.

Suzette watched him leave. Then, she grabbed the scissors off the tray. With everyone focused on the convulsing patient, she jumped at the Sergeant, driving the scissors deep into the side of his neck.

The Sergeant's body fell face-down over Jaylan.

The boy, tangled in his sheet, struggled under the Sergeant's weight and yelled, "Get him off me!"

A shadow rose above him as the black werewolf sailed over Jaylan's bed and the fallen Sergeant.

The boy twisted around and saw the huge and bloodied black wolf standing over the girl with her throat torn out.

Alexandria burst through the door. Wild-eyed she glanced from the murdered Sergeant to the murdered child, and her warning died within her.

Attendants eased Jaylan out from under Schwinn's body without hampering the surgeon's examination of the Sergeant. Nodding his head, the surgeon said, "He's gone."

"It all happened so fast," a nurse cried to Alexandria, "The child killed the Sergeant, and then the wolf killed the child!"

Freed, Jaylan pushed attendants away. He pointed at Jamaica and stammered, "H-he jumped over us: the cot, me, the Sergeant. He leapt right over us and k-killed her." He snapped at Alexandria, "Why didn't you see that would happen? Why didn't you stop it?"

The large wolf, with his ears back, padded out of the room. No one moved to stop him.

Leaning back against a wall, Alexandria cursed her uselessness and wept.

Every Marine in the room knew they would have to answer for what had happened to their Sergeant and to their prisoner: first to the Corps and, later, to a higher power.

Chapter 20

Loose Ends

The night the Sergeant and the ambusher's daughter died, Missy and Alexandria sat on the cots in their tent struggling to draft their article. Missy suggested, "What about the title, 'Human Ambushers Kill Marines'? That gives the reason for everything else that happened."

Alexandria mused, "That might be too sensational and narrow, but they need to know about human ambushers and the werewolves injured fighting for us. They need to know that dead child killed a Marine."

"The article has to be short enough for our bloggers to post."

"Alex, what about the title: 'A Tragedy Born of Hate'?"

"Better."

The two women wrote and rewrote their draft.

Alexandria mumbled, "We have to cut details in order to meet the word requirement."

Missy groaned, "Well, the truth without the details might . . . might what? Incite rage? Calm people? What?"

"The people who want a war with supernaturals will use anything we justify one."

"Let's read it again."

Outside, Akio and Johanna stood at a walkway railing. An alligator drifted through the channel, creating only a slight ripple in the water.

The taller Johanna, having a peach complexion and corn-silk blonde hair contrasted with the muscular Akio's black hair and Asian complexion. Yet, the witch's daughter and the samurai vampire shared a reverence for every nuanced sound around them. As they stood side-by-side, Akio said, "You are sad."

Johanna admitted, "It's about Linett. You fought in that Dohiyi battle, didn't you? Did you know my sister? Did you see her die?"

Softening his voice, he answered, "Your sister, like the rest of us vampires was resurrected dead. But, sweet girl, I did not see her final destruction. My brother and I fought zombies on the other side of a stand of trees."

Johanna touched his hand, saying, "If you read my thoughts, you'd know I'm not a sweet girl, anymore."

"I have been a vampire for over four-hundred years. Trust me that your thoughts would not shock me."

Knotting her long hair behind her head, she took a deep breath then started: "From the moment my twin disappeared, my parents started thinking of her as perfect. Overnight my identical twin's eyes became bluer than mine, her hair blonder, and her face 'angelic.' Even her music became magical—as though we hadn't played our violins together since we were five." Angry tears flowed as she said, "While she lived, we had no envy or pettiness between us. We took comfort in our mirrored existence. When she disappeared, I became the shadow of a ghost! But now, you can mesmerize me and take away my jealousy. You can help me love my sister the way I did before. Please, Akio."

Shaking his head, he said, "Linett's frozen in time, while you can move on and become more than what you were with her. Isamu and I are not identical, but we are twins. Our parents sent us to a sensei when we were very young. But Johanna, our parents are dust. Your jealousy will become dust if you leave it behind you."

Johanna looked away.

The next day, the perimeter guards allowed Captain James Nicci's armored command vehicle to enter through the main camp gate. Second Lieutenant John Ritt waited for him to disembark. Ritt's cobalt blue eyes and surfer-boy appeal showed none of the stress that came with the job. In contrast, Nicci's long face had grown haggard and his brown eyes blood-shot. The two officers saluted and fell into step, heading toward Ritt's command center.

Nicci asked, "How the hell did this happen, John?"

"The corpsman who removed Suzette's cuffs to treat her wounds rushed away to help a convulsing patient."

"And Sergeant Schwinn showed his back to a prisoner?"

"Schwinn showed his back to an undernourished, ten-year-old girl who had always been cuffed."

"The corpsman?"

"If he had a pattern of dereliction, I would recommend a court martial for failure to perform his duties. He doesn't. We're so short-staffed, I'll just demote him and let his supervisor decide if he should wash bedpans for a while."

"And the werewolf, Jamaica? According to your report, he killed that child. You also reported that the werewolf, Girl, threatened people. How are the rank and file responding to these attacks?"

"Sir, the ambushers wounded Marines and sent one of ours to his grave—while the werewolves scout for us here and ran ammunition to our squads through zombie herds. As far as I can tell, our people are on the wolves' sides."

The officers stopped on the walkway and gazed through the screening at the channel. The still water reflected blue sky. Along with the birds, frogs, and insects, came the sounds of Ulric's wooden Baroque flute and his melancholy song.

Nicci said, "In Dohiyi, I led this mix of humans and supernaturals. I know what the vampires and werewolves did for us then and do for us now. None of that makes it acceptable for them to attack and kill humans."

"If we arrest Jamaica for avenging Sergeant Schwinn, our truce with the werewolves might unravel."

"John, Schwinn's uncle is a senator. He's not going to accept a win/loss ratio as justification for his nephew's murder."

"With all due respect to the senator, war is a win/loss ratio—and this is a war."

Avianna's voice came from behind them. As Nicci worked to suppress his arousal, she gave him a knowing and seductive smile. "You have other problems, gentlemen," she purred.

"What now?" the Lieutenant asked.

"The werewolves are blockading."

"What?" Nicci demanded.

"They surrounded Girl's cot and will not allow more drugs to be administered."

His brow furrowed, Ritt asked, "Why now?"

Her Neapolitan accent thickened as she suggested, "Ah, but we cannot ask them. And, in my never-humble opinion, you should not punish the werewolves for doing what wolves do—protecting their canine and now human pack." She smiled and left them.

After she rounded a corner and disappeared, the two men, each lost in his own thoughts, made their way to the field hospital.

Four wolves filled the floor space around the comatose teenager's cot.

"The wolves," the chaplain assured the officers, "have not been aggressive with the doctors or staff, but the larger white one pulled the IV from the patient's arm. Now, they won't allow the doctors to reattach the sedative drip."

Nicci strode over to the doctors and asked about the medical risk of stopping the young werewolf's medications.

"She may experience fatigue and disorientation, but it won't last long."

"Then, let her wake up."

Ritt walked to Jaylan's cot. He noted the bags under the boy's eyes and his sagging shoulders, and asked, "How are you?"

Jaylan shrugged.

"I heard about your bravery, Son: that you stood in front of the prisoner to protect her from the wolf."

The boy squinted at him and groaned, "I'm an idiot. I should have let Girl eat her."

"You did the right thing. No one knew Suzette would kill the Sergeant and, in eight more years, I'm going to call on you to enlist."

Jaylan squinted at the officer. "What's going to happen to my father—for killing Suzette."

"It hasn't been decided."

The boy, although remembering Suzette's fear and grief, lied, "She deserved it." Sorrow for his own mother flooded through him. Then a flash of his father at the child's throat chilled him. He groaned, "It's all shit. These zombies have fucked up everything."

"Yes, they have."

When the boy did not continue, Ritt went to Shea.

The infection in her hand still discolored her fingers. She pulled her thick waves of red hair to the back of her neck but could not work a French knot.

Ritt started to reach for her hair to help her, but—remembering decorum—stopped himself. Instead, he lost himself in her green eyes.

Chapter 21

What Child Is This?

Under Lieutenant Ritt's scrutiny, Shea smiled.

"How are you?" he asked.

"I'm healing," she lied, "but I'm as sorry as Jaylan that we stood in front of that werewolf. If we had let Girl kill Suzette, the Sergeant would be alive now."

"You heard what I said to Jaylan. That goes for you, too."

"Lieutenant, someone's at fault."

"Yes, Miss Shea, but not you."

She gazed into his blue eyes and realized that, despite all that had happened, they remained the eyes of a young man. She wondered how he carried his responsibility then thought: my meemaw would have said, 'Bless your warrior heart.'

From the doorway, Nicci signaled Ritt to follow him outside. On the walkway, the Captain asked, "Whom do you want to promote to take Schwinn's place?"

"Coraggio."

"He's a good man. I'll try to find someone to fill his slot. The problem is that the world is less than forty percent what it was: including us."

Avianna approached them and asked, "And what have you decided about the werewolf—Jamaica?"

"Undecided," Nicci answered.

"We vampires and the werewolves have never trusted humans or each other. We fight for humanity with the expectation of betrayal. Your decision about Jamaica will prove us right or wrong."

"And what about the witches? Are they expecting betrayal?"

"As soon as people aren't seeing zombies on their front lawns, they'll fear the supernaturals who helped save them, but you need to be smarter. Decide about Jamaica gentlemen. *Decidere saggiamente*: decide wisely."

The two men watched her walk away and Ritt said, "The witches may have the scariest powers, but that vampire is pretty damn terrifying."

"One war at a time, James. We still have zombies to clear out. Let's check on Benwahr's line."

They made their way to the front of the camp, where Sergeant Barr Benwahr's front line, wore Hazmat suits and terminated the zombies drawn to their gunfire.

Nicci had just opened his mouth to address his Sergeant when the man jumped the T-wall.

Ritt yelled to the line, "Cease fire! Stop!"

All firing stopped as the front line tried to make sense of what was happening.

Benwahr bullied his way through the biters and swarms of flies around them. He snatched a small child who stumbled along the pavement.

The mud-covered toddler had not been crying but, scooped up by a man in all white with a glass face, she screamed.

The herd turned toward the sound and attacked.

Benwahr was average height but strong and held the squirming, screaming child above his head.

The biters surrounded him: ripping his hazmat suit and tearing into his flesh.

Nicci, Ritt, and the front line shot the zombies on the outside of the pack, but to shoot the ones ripping at their man would risk killing Benwahr and the child.

The samurai vampires appeared and broke through the front rank. With their katanas sweeping the air in bloody arks, they carved a path to the Marine and girl.

Isamu grabbed the child and held her against his chest with one arm, slicing at the pack with the katana in his other.

Akio threw the wounded Marine over his shoulder. Holding him with one arm, he swung the katana in the other. With slash after bloody slash, the brothers cleared a path.

Benwahr's people shot the zombies in the pack until the samurai leapt the wall.

Inside the barrier, two Marines took their Sergeant from Akio, while another took the child. The Marines rushed the patients to the hospital.

Nicci and Ritt approached the calm and undamaged vampires.

Nicci said, "Isamu, Akio, thank you."

Akio sighed and said, "We regret not reaching the Sergeant before he was injured, but we were on the other side of camp when we heard the ceasefire."

"From Dohiyi to this fight, you have never failed to help us when we needed it. But, if you'll excuse us, we want to see to our man."

Nicci and Ritt entered the hospital to find Benwahr strapped to a gurney.

His heavy lids half-covered green-gray eyes that sagged toward their outer corners. He had thick lashes, dark brows, and a long nose. His swarthy complexion had paled.

"You're a brave man, Sergeant," Nicci said.

"Thank you, sir. I wouldn't have made it back to the wall without the samurai."

"That only means you're braver."

"How's the baby?"

Nicci glanced over at the corpsman tending her.

The little girl may have been two years old. She had caramel skin, large brown eyes, and a halo of black curls. As a corpsman sang, "What Child is This?" the whimpering toddler quieted.

The Captain, without knowing the truth, assured his Sergeant, "She's going to be fine."

"I'll deploy to Aberdeen, sir?"

"Aberdeen will be your most important assignment, Barr."

"I know I'll become a lab rat, Captain. If experimenting on me helps them find a cure, it's okay."

Nicci rested his hand on the bound soldier's arm, too far from his mouth to be bitten. "Your sacrifice will not be forgotten," he said, "and we'll send your tags and purple heart to your family."

Benwahr's eyes glazed and his speech slowed: "No family left . . . left. Keep medal . . . tags. For. . . baby."

A fly landed on the Sergeant's bandaged shoulder. With a flash of loathing, Nicci swatted, caught, and crushed the bug.

Ritt reached for Benwhar's shoulder--then pulled back his hand. He knew better than to come close to a bitten-man's teeth. "The nearest orphanage is in Coral Gables," he explained, "so I'll do what I can to make sure they save your medal for when the girl is older."

The Sergeant struggled to say, "Samurai."

"Yes, I'll ask the samurai instead."

"Trust."

"Yes."

"Warriors . . . honoral . . . Marine . ."

Nicci touched his leg, above a bandage through which blood still seeped. He assured him, "Yes they're honorable warriors, like us."

"Lab," the man repeated.

Nicci responded, "I've received an official report that they're closer to a vaccine. You'll bring them even closer. Rest now." The Captain nodded toward the door. He and Ritt left together.

Outside, somewhere among the tents, a Marine sang, "Swing Low Sweet Chariot." Despite his being off-key, the words comforted Nicci.

Avianna and Joseph, with Isamu and Akio, waited nearby.

Avianna said, "Give the samurai Benwahr's tags and medal. They will track where the child goes and give them to her when she's older."

Nicci frowned and asked, "Is there anything you don't hear?"

Without her usual playfulness, Avianna answered, "*Non tanto:* not much. Too often, I hear more than I want to know."

The vampires left, heading toward their tents, but the commanding officers lingered, discussing the promotion of Creole Vanyan into Benwahr's place. Creole was in a different squad, but he was a sharpshooter with more military experience than the people under Benwahr.

Since neither Nicci nor Ritt wanted to be alone, they walked together to the end of a raised walkway. From there, they watched two alligators sleeping on the opposite bank.

Chapter 22

Sibling Rivalry

The next morning, Kahl-maus's two teenage creations sat at the chipped enamel table in their battered camper. Scraps of fabric and sheets of newspaper blocked the windows.

Starved and shriveled with her eyes yellowed, Eve groaned, "Remember Father's grand plan to have us turn a hundred children into a vampire army for him?"

"Yeah."

Eve pushed her thin brown hair out of her eyes and sniped, "Well, we botched that didn't we? We either failed in their creation or made them so mindless we had to put them down. Father's great army is just you and me."

"He'll be happy with our putting that child in the zombie herd."

"We're desperate and needed that child's blood. I hate Father's power over us, and I hate calling him Father. He was turned when he was our age: fifteen. It's so frustrating."

"He created us, and he's been a vampire for over nine-hundred years! You didn't complain when he hunted for us before the witch locked him into mist."

"We can hunt for ourselves now."

"But Father's right. If we take a Marine, Avianna will come after us."

"So, Father won't let us take a Marine, but why not take another kid from a development near the 'glades? After we drink the bodies dry, the rotters will destroy them."

Adam rolled his eyes and pushed his hand through his short, dark hair. Groaning, he said, "Father ordered, 'No direct attacks.' Defying him is impossible."

Eve twisted her hair around a jittery finger then said, "Avianna defies Father. Why don't we ask her how."

"He says she'll end us."

"She's our big sister."

"She'll end us, Eve. Remember that every vampire we've ever met says Avianna Riardi's an aberration; the only one they know who can defy her sire. She won't see herself as our sister."

"Okay, but I'm so hungry, Adam!"

A thought entered both their minds at the same time: "I am here."

The teenagers turned toward the only open window. There, a black mist seeped inside then hovered under the low ceiling.

Through their link, Kahl-maus said, "I will go with you into the nearest neighborhood so you can feed. You must be quick and not be seen. Cover yourselves, and let us go, now."

That evening, under a full moon, bats circled high above Avianna. Discomforted and watchful, the tall and lithe vampire walked the perimeter of the camp. When she came to the front T-wall, she stood beside a guard. She pushed her long black hair to her back where it hung to her waist.

Together, the vampire and guard scanned the snarling zombie herd on the circular driveway and front lawn. The herd included less than one-third the number of biters than what had come months before. Amidst them, a dark woman with textured layers of burgundy hair, wore a yellow summer dress with a princess neckline. Her skin still had a sheen of perspiration and her wounds still bled profusely. She clutched yellow heels as though she had taken them off to run and forgotten she still carried them. Avianna reached into the woman's mind. She found only hunger and control over mobility.

The guard next to the vampire hesitated.

"*Morta*," she told him, "nothing left."

The guard fired and the woman dropped, attracting the attention of the nearest zombies. Three of them tore into her still healthy flesh. The Marines took down the attacking biters.

Avianna left the wall and strode the walkway to the hospital where she found Joseph helping patients. She led him outside.

"What's wrong?"

"My sire is in the Everglades, and two more vampires are in the area. They may all be together. Kahl-maus can't do much as mist, but others helping him would be bad. I'm telling you because he would love hurting someone I love. I also need to tell Akio and Isamu." She kissed, then embraced Joseph, murmuring, "Be careful, my love." Without another word, she hastened to find her friends.

On her way to their tent, she stopped, listened to the sounds in the swamp, and changed direction. Moving west on the outermost walkway, she paused at a place from which insects and small creatures had fled. The black mist rose and hovered.

She glared at him and said, "Ah, *falso padre*, have you brought friends? Oh. Wait, There is a connection. Have you created *mio fratello e mia sorella*—a brother and sister for me?"

Through the sire bond, she heard 'yes.'

"*I loro nomi*—their names, Kahl-maus?"

"Adam and Eve."

"Why have you come to me?"

"To ask you not to hurt them.'

"What have they done that I would hurt them?"

A whiff of his malevolence reached her.

She sighed, "Ahhhh, I know you. They placed the child in the herd to have Marines die trying to save her."

'You have killed more, daughter.'

"*Si*, I have killed countless more—the worst I could find. But why are you distracting me with this nonsense?"

Scuffling sounds caught Avianna's attention. Then came screams from different parts of camp. One voice she recognized. Forgetting Kahl-maus, she ran toward it.

Through their sire-bond, Joseph said, 'I'm coming, Avianna.'

By the time Avianna reached eighteen-year-old Shea, the girl struggled under a groping, jaw-snapping zombie who bit into the forearm of her injured hand. Shea's scream became a continuous wail. While the young warrior punched the zombie with her good hand, the creature gnawed on the still healthy flesh above her infection. Bleeding out, Shea lacked the strength to push him away.

Avianna grabbed the zombie's head but tearing it away might take the girl's arm with it. Grumbling Italian curses, the vampire held the zombie's hair with one hand and reached under his chin with the other to rip away his lower jaw.

Shea passed out.

Alligators in the shallow water below the walkway snapped at the blood that dripped between the slats.

Still cursing in Italian, the vampire clamped her hands around Shea's arm above the damage and stemmed the flow of the virus to Shea's brain.

Appearing beside her, Joseph pulled tools from his medical bag saying, "I'll take her arm!"

Shea woke, flailing in pain.

Avianna called her name and captured the young woman's attention. The vampire's luminous green eyes filled Shea's vision.

The wounded fighter's pulse slowed, and her pain became a distant echo.

While Avianna kept eye contact and her tourniquet-grip, Joseph did the work of three surgeons.

A crowd squeezed onto the narrow walkway. Hospital corpsman pushed their way to the front and froze, astounded by the procedure in front of them. The chief surgeon shoved past the corpsman, but Keenu blocked his path.

"Interfere," the witch said, "and I'll fuse your fingers to each other."

As soon as Joseph tied the last stitch, Avianna lifted the unconscious girl. The crowd parted, and—faster than a human eye perceived—the vampire sped Shea to the hospital. Medical personnel scrambled to follow.

Akio and three Marines had already run with Mary and Kristian toward the scream on the eastern side of the camp. Isamu and two Marines had run with Jamaica and Elderwolf toward the scream on the western side.

Isamu reached a shrieking nurse and yanked a zombie off her. Marines lifted the dying woman and ran her back to the hospital, while Isamu rolled the now beheaded zombie under the screening. Jamaica and Elderwolf ran along the fencing, snarled at the swamp where Adam ran away.

On the other side of camp, Akio found a Marine in the grip of a taller rotter. The young man twisted his face and neck away from the creature's bite and fired his handgun over his shoulder into the zombie's forehead. The zombie dropped.

Mary and Kristian ran along the fencing howling at Eve as she fled.

Akio said, "Let me see," and examined the man's shoulder. Then he assured the man, "You are not bitten. The gunfire burned your neck, and your ear bleeds from percussion."

As Akio rolled the zombie under the screening and into the marsh below, a Marine asked, "How the hell did those rotters get through the screening and over the rails?"

The other pointed toward the snapping werewolves and said, "Someone lifted these rotters, and the wolves saw where they ran"

Isamu, Akio, and the wolves met at the hospital, where Avianna waited outside. She told the others, "The nurse is dead. The Marine will be fine. Shea may not survive. Joseph and the Second Lieutenant are with her."

Akio nodded and said, "Lieutenant Ritt has strong *kanjo* for the young Miss."

Having known the samurai for over four-hundred years, Avianna understood the Japanese word for 'love.' She grinned and said, "Yes, but it is very human to wait too long for the right love, or rush into the wrong one."

Isamu started to respond, but Akio interrupted, saying, "Those zombies were lifted under the screening and over the rail onto the walkway. That took strength and no fear of being bitten."

"*Sì*, Kahl-maus is here with two other vampires."

Isamu nodded, "Do you want our help, my friend?"

"No. He is my sire and they are my siblings: my responsibilities. But they can wait until I make time for them."

As Henry approached, he asked, "Who can wait?"

Isamu and Akio left Avianna with the newcomer they distrusted.

Alone with Avianna, Henry continued, "Are you planning the destruction of another innocent? One like Linett?"

"*Io miei affair:* my business with my sire. If you had been a better sire, Henry, Linett would not have come with us."

Henry snapped, "And if you had not blocked my commands, I would have forced her to return to the safety of my nest." Then he added,

"Whatever you're going to do, Avianna Riardi, make sure you survive it. When all this is done, you and I have a final date."

Not responding, Avianna walked away.

Chapter 23

Blessings and Curses

The dark sky forced the physicians and staff in the makeshift camp hospital to turn on every light. In the still shadowy room. corpsmen took Shea's vitals and gave her a blood transfusion. An attendant handed Joseph clean scrubs so he could shower and change without returning to his tent. He set them aside for later and stayed to keep watch over the girl. Side-by-side, he and the surgeon supervised Shea's care.

Dropping his previous animosity, the pale and thin chief surgeon told Joseph, "Remarkable work, Doctor."

Built like a middleweight, with light brown hair and hazel eyes, Joseph accepted the compliment and responded, "We'll know when she wakes if her mind is still clear."

"If I hadn't watched you vampires drink the blood donations, I might want to be one of you—just to be able to operate like that."

Joseph faced the man and said, "Avianna makes my existence bearable. She is the reason I didn't walk this dead shell into the sunlight the first week. She helps me stay close to who I was. With the wrong sire, a vampire can become a vile predator."

The surgeon, keeping distance between himself and the bound girl, said, "If Shea's mind alters, we'll have to transport her to Aberdeen."

"Shea's not a Marine. Avianna and I will take her back to her hometown to be buried."

The surgeon sighed and said, "Please believe that I hate sending my patients to the Aberdeen labs, but you're a doctor and a scientist. You know that we only have a promise of a vaccine because of the research done on victims."

Different branches of the military plowed through zombies from coast-to-coast, while Joseph did research in European and U.S. labs. He knew kind scientists and cruelly insensitive ones but kept this history to himself.

While the doctors talked, Lieutenant Ritt left to supervise Marines and supernaturals boarding the airboats. His helmet hid his blond hair, and the dark clouds kept sunshine out of his cobalt-blue eyes.

His mind drifted back to Shea's fight for survival, and he wondered why the witch hadn't helped her. The witch had manipulated wind, water, and earth—and locked the werewolves into their wolf forms. But he had heard that changing a sentient being takes black magic. He murmured, "Maybe black magic scares even her."

The rumble of swampbuggies reached him, and the loss of Schwinn tightened Ritt's nerves. He and the Sergeant had come up through the ranks together. Both were in the battle for Dohiyi. They had eaten together, slept in the same tent, and sat side-by side to clean their weapons. Now, it was Coraggio's responsibility to bring Schwinn's squad, Hilanor, Alexandria, and the werewolves back alive.

On the trail, Sergeant Coraggio and his people reached the far side of the burned area. Alexandria touched the Sergeant's shoulder, saying, "Wait. There's a large herd ahead."

The Sergeant signaled the buggies to stop and the Marines to form a wedge. Running ahead of the squad, the wolves located the herd. As the biters surged toward them, the wolves ran in a circle to keep the pursuing herd jumbled in the center. The wolves howled to help Coraggio identify the battle perimeter.

When the Marines opened fire, Kristian led his pack to the swampbuggies and under them. Although the werewolves could survive normal bullets, they did not court injury.

Black storm clouds churned above them and unleashed torrential rain. Hilanor stood and spread his arms. His deep voice vibrated as he pointed upward and intoned,

Nature's power feed my own,
To drive away the winds you've blown,

He focused on the sky until a wind gusted against the swirling clouds and rolled them away from the battle. The roiling sky, caught by new currents, drifted to the Marine's encampment and the surrounding mangroves. There, its fury unleashed—forcing the boats to return earlier than planned.

In camp, Avianna pulled Joseph away from his patient, and then she whispered, "I must stop Kahl-maus's other children. This storm makes it easier for me to slip away."

"You are not alone. Girl slipped away about an hour ago. We all expected her to wake enraged, but she left without a sound while everyone around her slept.

"I need to leave without Henry's curiosity. Can you check the werewolf tents for her?"

He wondered why Henry mattered, but said, "Go, before the storm breaks."

With thunder and lightning as cover, she climbed down the ladder to the loading dock. Without rocking the boats, she leapt from moored boat to moored boat until her last leap took her into the swamp.

The swirling black mist drifted out from the foliage to cover signs of a trail. Through his connection to his oldest creation, Kahl-maus implored, 'Please, daughter, they're innocent.'

Tall and willowy, with her raven hair dripping water to her waist, Avianna strode through her sire's non-corporeal form.

'Daughter! I taught them what I knew: to hunt the weakest of humans!" When Avianna did not respond, he tried again: "My sire created me when I was young. Then, he left. He cared as little for me as my human parents had.'

"You made Adam and Eve kill—not to feed, but to devil me as you always have."

His mind cried, 'Do not take my only faithful children from me! Do not leave me alone in this helpless form!' She did not respond, and he swirled over the roots and moss, reaching through his bond with Adam and Eve to warn them of Avianna's approach. He allowed their panic to fill his mind and flow to his oldest creation.

Avianna moved through thigh-deep water and rotted undergrowth as though they were air. She atomized into mist to pass through a large patch of thick brush, reforming on the other side. Bats chittered above her and insects fled her cold skin.

Kahl-maus begged, 'If I promise to never bother you again, will you let us leave?'

"*Dispettoso!*" she shouted, "Spiteful boy! For nine-hundred years you have had the hungers of a vampire with the mind of willful child —and, this time, you used other children to do great harm!"

'I promise to stay away with them."

"You cannot keep that promise! You are selfish and vengeful and will plague me until I ask the witch to change you back, just so I can end you!"

'But you and Joseph will perish with me!"

"*Sì,* "she agreed, "*Se devo*—if I must; if you make that the only way to stop your malevolence."

Refocusing on her siblings, the vampire strode through him again.

Fifteen minutes later, Avianna emerged from the swamp several yards from Adam's and Eve's camper. With a wave of her hand, the bats that had followed her settled in the highest branches of the trees. She blocked Kahl-maus's pleas and listened for the teenagers.

A volley of bullets buzzed the air. Graceful and assured, the oldest sister shifted and they missed. Again, and again, she leaned to the right, the left, twisted, or dashed until her siblings stopped firing. The whistle of a projectile warned her. Its glass shattered against the ground and burst into flames. A second, a third, and a fourth cocktail ignited patches of grass. Breezes spread the fires across the lawn.

Chapter 24

Alienation

'Where is she?' Adam shouted to Eve.

From where she hid, his sister yelled back, 'I don't know.'

"*Sono qui*," Avianna said from behind Adam.

He spun to strike but her open palm propelled him upward.

He hit the lawn and skidded through the burning grass. Screaming, he rose with his clothes ablaze.

Eve ran to him and dragged him, at vampire speed, into a nearby brook. Steam billowed in the air around them. She left Adam cooling in the water., With blistering skin on her arms and face, she came ashore crying with pain and rage.

Avianna appeared before her and grasped the front of the teenager's shirt in one fist. She lifted the cursing girl.

"You're not fighting humans," Eve screamed. She clutched both sides of her older sister's head and pushed her thumbs into the woman's eyes.

Avianna's eyes turned to mist, and she grabbed Eve's hips and flipped the girl over her head onto the grass behind her. The teenager crashed to the ground but leapt to her feet and lunged at the older vampire's back.

With her luminous eyes reformed, Avianna spun toward Eve. She lifted the girl above her head and flung her toward a large oak tree.

Twisting in the air, the younger vampire grasped a limb instead of crashing into the trunk.

Adam, a half-naked patchwork of burns, rose screaming from the water and charged Avianna from behind. She disappeared. He grabbed air, and then found himself in an unbreakable chokehold.

Eve shrieked and the colony of bats dispersed with rapid chitter that sounded like screeching. To save her brother the girl ran at full speed into Avianna's outstretched fist. The closed fist punctured the girl's chest, splintered her ribs, and ruptured her right lung. Eve pulled back stunned and stared at the stolen blood gushing from the hole. She collapsed, weeping, "Please, Sister, we cannot disobey our sire."

Tears rimed Avianna's eyes as she said, "I know." On that last word, she took hold of both sides of Adam's head and twisted. With shock and pain still on his young face, she tore his neck from his body, then tossed his body and head onto the burning lawn.

Eve staggered to her feet. Crying, "I hate you!" she snatched a fallen tree branch and jabbed it toward her older sibling's heart.

Avianna angled away from the blow, and the branch scraped her shoulder. She yanked the makeshift spike from Eve's grasp and held onto it.

Still bleeding, Eve stumbled backward.

Avianna caught her and, trembling, with her voice barely a hiss, she said, "You missed your mark. The shaft belongs here." With that, she plunged the branch into the girl's heart.

Eve dropped. What little blood remained trickled from both wounds. Eve's body began to dry and shrivel.

The older sister knelt and cradled the younger like an infant. She stroked her hair, saying, "I mourn all you might have been." To stop the girl's slow and painful degradation, Avianna broke her neck and spinal cord. Then she carried Eve to the nearest blaze. Ignoring the flames that blistered her arms Avianna lay the girl in the fire.

When the ashes of her siblings mixed with the ashes of the lawn, no one would guess vampires perished there. Their sad stories would end with their having run away from home a decade before.

Knowing residents of the nearest houses would see flames against the night sky, Avianna disappeared into the trees.

As siren wails filled the air, the black mist followed her. His deep despair flooded through their sire-bond. Though agonized, he could not cry in the form of mist.

"Kahl-maus," his oldest creation groaned, "I am sorry for your broken mind and darkened soul, but *non piu*: no more! You killed and turned me over eight centuries ago. Now, you have killed children and pitted them against me. You have remained base and low. Now, *stammi lontano*: stay away from me!" With that, she strode into the swamp. This time, Kahlmaus did not follow.

Avianna's mind replayed images of the destruction she had wrought, and her tears flowed. Curling and uncurling her fists, her blue veins showed through pale skin. She needed a place to stop where she did not have to think or feel. Ignoring the alligators who watched from nearby, she left the trail that led back to the encampment.

Desperate for solitude, she strode through the mire to a majestic bald cypress. Draped in Spanish moss, its limbs spread twenty feet around. Its woody knees rose five feet above clear water, and its trunk rose a hundred-and-twenty-feet to the sky. No other tree grew in its shadow.

Avianna touched the gray bark with gentle fingertips before climbing halfway. As the sun rose, she nestled into a deep and shadowed fork. She leaned against the peeling bark, kissed the tips of soft, feathery needles, and sighed.

For a long, deep, and healing sleep, she needed her native soil, but being more metaphysical than physical, she could ease her mind and spirit without it. She closed her eyes and allowed Joseph to know she survived. Then, with every intention to stay through that day and the next night, she closed her eyes and quieted her sorrowful mind.

Chapter 25

Fury and Trust

Jaylan sat by Shea's bed, reading to her from a crumpled magazine. His dreadlocks draped in front of his face.

The injured young warrior opened her eyes to the afternoon sun outside the hospital windows. Jaylan's sad smile moved her to reach for him, but the blanket did not shift. She had been tucked in tightly. Again, she thought she pulled on the sheet, but it stayed in place.

Perspiring, she choked out, "I remember the attack. I was bitten! I'm infected!"

"No, Shea. No."

She closed her eyes, and the snapping zombie tore into her again. She flinched and insisted, "I have to be infected."

"You're not a rotter. You wouldn't be able to question me if you were."

"How is this possible?"

Jaylan leaned close and whispered, "Keenu went to D.C. and came back with vaccine—only enough for five of us. She gave them to you, me, Alexandria, Missy, and a Marine. No one else can know."

Shea whispered back, "How did she get it?"

"I don't know. I only know they're not telling people because there isn't enough."

Shea closed her green eyes and reviewed all that she knew about the infection. When she opened her eyes, Joseph stood by Jaylan's chair. Tears flowed as she reasoned, "Too fast! I would have been infected before the vaccine could get here."

Jaylan searched for the right words and failed.

Resting a hand on the boy's shoulder, Joseph said, "Jaylan, you're exhausted and need food and sleep. Doctor's orders: go to the galley and let me talk to my patient."

Jaylan nodded, kissed Shea's cheek, and left the room. Instead of going to the galley, he hovered outside, listening through an open window.

"Joseph," Shea said, "tell me--now."

"A zombie bit you, and we needed to stop the spread of the infection."

"I remember Avianna's squeezing my arm."

"She stopped the blood-flow."

Shea stretched the bitten arm without the sheet moving. Shivering, she gasped, "Tell me the rest."

In a quiet, firm voice, Joseph said, "I removed your arm above the elbow, Shea." He waited for her to grasp the enormity of what he had done.

A wave of nausea shook the girl and she trembled. "I should be angry," she said, "and afraid."

"I operated outside. Avianna worked within your mind during the surgery to help you survive it. Now, drugs are helping to dull the pain; but your courage, Shea, that's all you."

The eighteen-year-old's face paled. With only one arm, she was useless—to the Marines in camp and to the militia at home.

The rotter drooled on her face. She bit her lips and twisted her face away from his snapping jaws. He tore flesh from her arm, and she screamed.

Joseph's warm voice pulled her back into the hospital room: "Shea." As she focused on him, he assured her, "You have flashbacks, but you're okay."

"My spider bite hadn't healed."

The Marine surgeon appeared beside Joseph and said, "Your hand was not healing, Shea."

"You would've taken my hand?"

"Yes. If the zombie bite hadn't forced the amputation of your arm, you would have lost that hand."

On a signal from the Marine surgeon, a corpsman injected Shea's damaged arm just below the shoulder.

"Sleep now," Joseph suggested, "and I'll try to persuade Jaylan to sleep, too. He hasn't left your side since this happened."

"I need to talk to him again. Can y'all find him for me?"

"We've given you an analgesic and sedative. You might not be able to stay awake."

"Then, talk to me, Joseph, while we wait for him to come back."

From the doorway, Jaylan asked, "Until who comes back?"

"You," Shea said, "We need a talk."

In a shrill voice he asked, "What's happened?"

Backing away from the cot, Joseph said, "Nothing more, Jaylan. She's strong."

The other surgeon left with Joseph, and Jaylan took a seat. In a shaky attempt to sound normal, he said, "So, what's up?"

"I'm going on back to Dohiyi. They'll prescribe physical therapy, and that's where I want to have it. My meemaw used to say, 'Bless the hearts of tourists and fools.' Their hunting and skiing accidents paid for our little hospital to have the best equipment."

Jaylan groaned, "You're leaving?"

She cleared her throat and said, "I have to go on home and face my brother."

"What do you mean 'face' him?"

"I'm so much like your father and you."

"You can't be like both of us."

"Yes, I am, Jaylan. While I was with the militia, zombies took my parents and bit my little sister. So, like your pa, I didn't save my family. And yes, the way you killed your mama, I killed my sister. My brother survived; but, like your dad, I left."

Jaylan rubbed the back of his neck and stuttered, "Y-y-you left him? Like m-m-my father left me?"

"After I let our parents die and after I killed our sister, facing my brother became impossible."

"Cowards. You and my dad are cowards."

"I want to help you understand your father . . . and me."

"Bullshit! You're just making excuses for both of you."

"I'm sorry."

Jaylan sprang from the chair, knocking it to the floor, and shouted, "You're only defending my father because you did the same thing. That's not friendship." He fled the room and the door slammed behind him.

Not wanting the Marines to see her cry, Shea used her remaining hand to cover her face with the blanket. Then she let the meds and exhaustion close her eyes.

Jaylan ran to the end of the longest walkway and watched for the patrol boats returning.

A man helping to tie the boats spoke to a group of disembarking Marines. The group glared across the short distance at Jaylan.

Muscular, six-foot-tall Kowolski marched up to the boy saying, "Hey, kid!" He removed his helmet, uncovering his regulation cut, sandy-blond hair.

Jaylan glanced at the man's stripes and asked, "Yes, Sergeant?"

"I hear you gave our girl, Shea, a tough time."

"That's between me and her."

"Wrong, kid. Miss Shea covered our asses in Dohiyi, and she's been sticking her pretty, little neck out here. The way you treat her is between you and the whole damn Corps, boy."

Caramel complexioned Jaylan snapped, "Don't call me, 'boy'."

"Don't knot your knickers, kid. About everyone in town, called me 'boy' at your age. My father still does."

On the narrow walkway the eleven-year-old stood as a sapling in the shadow of a mighty oak. He braced himself and grumbled, "I ain't your kid, your boy, your son, or your nothing." He kept it to himself that he did not know the meaning of the word, knickers.

Kowolski growled, "You treat us with respect—and that includes everyone who fights beside us, or you'll end up a long-tailed cat in a room filled with rocking chairs. You got that, Mister Savann?"

Stifling his anger toward Shea and his father, Jaylan murmured, "I never meant to disrespect the Corps."

"Good."

An egret in flight caught the boy's attention. Its tranquility soothed him.

Before Kowolski could say more, Keenu's voice came from behind him. "Is there a problem, Sergeant?" she asked.

The Marine frowned at the powerful witch and said, "No ma'am. The boy and I are just talking."

"Well Sergeant, I also have something to discuss with Jaylan."

"Then I'll leave you to it, ma'am."

Keenu turned sideways to let the Marine pass and then faced the boy and said, "I understand that you're angry at your papa and Shea."

"So?"

The witch's eyebrows furrowed and all their garments ruffled in a new breeze. She squinted at the boy and said, "Attitude, Jaylan!"

"Sorry."

"I'm asking about your being angry because I'm still angry at Avianna and Hilanor over my daughter's death. I met Avianna right before Dohiyi and did not know her well, but Hilanor and I have been friends for a long time. I expected him to be honest with me."

"What did they do?"

"Avianna brought Linett into the battle for Dohiyi, but my beautiful, musical child didn't have the fighting skills to survive a zombie horde. Hilanor blocked my ability to sense that a doll we used in spell-casting represented my daughter."

"Why did they do that?"

"Avianna said it was Linett's choice and Hilanor claimed he needed to keep me focused on the battle. Their excuses don't help me anymore than your papa's and Shea's excuses help you."

Jaylan leaned back against the railing and, avoiding eye-contact, grumbled. "Yeah. Wrong shit is wrong shit."

"Now, I don't know how to forget their betrayals."

"But you're a witch. You can turn your two into snails or something. All I can do is hate mine."

"But my daughter loved Hilanor and Avianna, so Linett wouldn't want me hurting them."

Jaylan remembered his mother and father nestled together on the couch. He could still hear their laughter. His mother might not want him hating his father, either. Struggling to hold back tears, he stayed quiet.

"Sounds like we both have to figure out how to forgive what we can't forget."

He nodded.

Keenu stood in front of him and said, "Jaylan, I can't hug my Linett anymore, and I miss her hugs like crazy. Would you mind if I hugged you?"

He stepped closer.

The mother of three opened her arms and the eleven-year-old slipped into her embrace. She kissed the top of his head.

He tightened his arms around her waist, surprised that he did not want to let go. Then, realizing he had let the witch into a private place in his heart, he broke off the embrace and ran. He sprinted to the hospital tent to retrieve his backpack. Then he dashed to the werewolf section where he found Elderwolf and Jamaica, already sleeping on the ground outside their tents.

Girl opened the flap and said, "Hello. Mary and Kristian have the other tent, so you're in here with me."

"I thought you were still in the hospital."

"As soon as I woke, I slipped out. I needed to stop their pumping me full of anti-psycho drugs because I'm not crazy. I know who I hate and why, and it's not you or my werewolf family."

He dropped his backpack and plopped down onto the nearest blanket, saying. "How did you know I would come?"

"Alexandria."

Too tired to answer, he sighed and closed his eyes.

Girl asked, "How's Shea?"

"Probably sleeping."

"You want your dad in here?"

The werewolf's son shook his head.

Girl stood for a minute, thinking, 'This boy, this human child, closes his eyes and sleeps in my tent.' His trust comforted her. Then, she left for the galley and—her mood shifting—she mumbled, "I hope Keenu's not there. She's too dangerous for me to fight. Hell, she's too dangerous to be allowed to live."

Chapter 26

Relative Risks

When Girl first joined the pack, Kristian insisted she train with rifles, knives, and pistols. He wanted all the werewolves to be able to protect themselves and their communities while in human form. With those skills, First Squad might accept her.

At sunrise, she headed toward the armory but met Keenu on the way. Girl stopped the witch to say, "Alexandria told me you brought vaccines for the youngest people here. I'm younger than your daughter and her friend. Why didn't I get one, or is it too obvious?"

Keenu touched the teenager's arm and said. "I'm sorry, Girl. Without having seen an infected werewolf, we don't know if you're vulnerable."

"So, we're half-human and on the front lines, but we don't get vaccinated?"

"I've been told that your super-healing might attack the vaccine."

"And no one's dissected a werewolf to find out? After you stole my ability to change, why not have me dissected, too?"

Keenu shuddered at having blocked the young werewolf's ability to change but focused on the vaccine: "Supernaturals only went public after Dohiyi."

"What happens to us if no one does the research? We never get vaccinated?"

Keenu thought about the risks the werewolves took and swallowed hard. Researchers might not confirm werewolf immunity to prevent a worldwide hunt for Lycan blood. On the other side, they might withhold verification of werewolf vulnerability to keep the wolves on the front line. "I'm sorry, Girl," Keenu said, "but I haven't been told anything." As Girl passed her, the witch touched gentle fingers to the teen's shoulder, but Girl pulled away.

Then Keenu sighed and headed for the command tent. As she entered, Lieutenant Ritt glanced at her clothing. Irregular lines of golden embroidery, like the thinnest branches at the top of a tree, reached from the hemline to the neckline. The fabric beneath the embroidery came close to the color of her dark complexion. "Must you wear those clothes?" he snapped, "This is a war, not a cotillion."

"And I'm not a soldier," she snapped back then deflected to, "You asked to see me."

Ritt calmed himself. Then, he poured two cups of coffee and handed her one. Then he said, "Explain the vaccine. Rumor is that you commandeered a helicopter, flew to DC, and stole vaccines. I need the truth, Miss Keenu, and DON'T trash this tent again!"

She grimaced and snarled, "Don't act like the sun comes up just to hear you crow. I don't take kindly to being yelled at."

Instead of apologizing, Ritt frowned.

The witch sighed and said, "Alexandria gave me a cell phone she and Missy collected, and I called Senator Schwinn. He sent a helicopter to pick me up in the supermarket parking lot a mile away, but I needed a little witchcraft to get through the zombies." When Ritt did not interrupt, she continued, "In his D.C. office, the senator gave me his and his wife's doses. Three of his staff volunteered their vaccines, too. All five said they are surrounded by security and wanted people on the front lines to have their shots."

"All this happened without your telling me?"

"He wanted me to hand them to Joseph before letting anyone know we had them."

"Joseph? The vampire instead of my chief surgeon?"

"Avianna and Joseph, Kristian and Mary, and me—we all met the senator before Dohiyi. He's the one who took our offer of supernatural help to the president."

"Miss Keenu, bloggers are calling that first meeting 'a historic summit."

"After the meeting, Dohiyi was chosen as the test site for a supernatural/human coalition."

"And that's how your group came to fight alongside us there?"

"Yes. The senator knows that Joseph doesn't need the vaccine for himself. He also knows that I wouldn't steal doses when I can steal shipments."

Ritt winced at the reminder of the witch's power and asked, "So, Joseph administered the shots?"

"He gave them to the four youngest—Jaylan, Shea, Missy, and Alexandria. The senator asked that one dose go to a Marine who fought beside his nephew, so Joseph gave a dose to someone in that squad."

"Girl is younger than your daughter and Missy, so I'm guessing the doctors don't know if the vaccine will work on a werewolf. Wait! You're saying that a Marine accepted a dose without having enough for his squad?"

The witch answered, "Joseph didn't tell anyone, including the Marine. The man or woman doesn't know that the vaccine was in the shot. Even I don't know who Joseph vaccinated."

Ritt poured himself another cup. Then huffed, "Okay."

The radio operator from Louisiana—the one the others called 'T'—opened the tent flap. He bent his tall, wiry frame to lean inside and say, "Beggin' your pardon, Lieutenant."

Recognizing the man who played guitar and sang old war songs for the others in camp, Ritt asked, "Yes, Sergeant?"

The young man handed a missive to Ritt and explained, "There's an urgent message for you from Senator Schwinn. It's marked 'private,' sir." He nodded toward the witch. Born and reared in New Orleans, he had met other women who claimed to be witches and learned to spot the charlatans. This one was different. She could move wind, water, and earth; this one was real. He visualized Keenu Kulae in a graveyard under a bright moon. He shivered but said, "Ma-am."

Keenu smiled and said, "Sergeant."

Reading the message, Ritt mumbled, "Dismissed." After 'T' left, Ritt waved the note at Keenu and said, "The senator confirms everything you said. He also convinced others to donate their doses to military children in their districts. Did you have anything to do with that?"

"No, Lieutenant, but an airboat's waiting for me. I need to change into something sensible, don't I?"

"Yes, you do."

Keenu left Ritt at his desk, staring at a different communiqué he had received the night before. That one instructed him to submit a report about the strengths and weaknesses of each kind of supernatural. Assuming headquarters wanted the information for a future war with them, Ritt grumbled, "Damn." He would have to report that the witch's control over the elements made her and others like her the most dangerous of the supernaturals. On the other side, the humanity of the witches and warlock, and their human families, made peace important to them. He pushed the paper aside. He needed time to think about how to word his response.

In a moment of synchronicity, a Marine passing Ritt's tent said, "I'm still not okay with all this."

The man's companion answered, "Yeah, the witch can do big-ass damage, but that sexy vampire scares me more. The way she ripped off heads in Dohiyi? Man! I like mine where it is."

Inside the tent, Ritt grunted in agreement.

Chapter 27

Vampire Regrets

Unseen as she passed through camp, Avianna slipped into her tent.

Joseph rose from his cot and rushed to embrace her. He whispered into her neck, "That took almost two days! The sun's coming up. How far did you track Kahl-maus's other children?"

Avianna eased out of his arms and said, "Adam and Eve circled through the swamp to where they had hidden a camper. After I destroyed them, I needed time to myself."

"You blocked me from your thoughts."

"Kahl-maus sired them—that made them my siblings. I did not want you sharing my thoughts."

"How old?"

"Barely teens. I have never killed young people before."

"Vampires, Avianna—already dead. No different from us."

"Kahl-maus raised them wrong."

"You left him and taught yourself."

"Joseph, a flaw in our bond let me leave him. They could not."

He kissed her shoulder and said, "Linett had a strong sire bond with Henry, but she left him."

"We found her in time for me to block their connection. We kept her moving around the world, always ahead of him, but her staying with us, *amore mio*: that's why she perished in Dohiyi." She softened her voice and added, "*Mi dispiace*. I'm sorry to remind you that, beneath our love, you are bound to me."

"I love you so deeply that I do not feel the sire-bond."

"Your love masks it, but it is there."

Joseph's face whitened and blue veins showed through his pale skin, but Avianna had already turned away and begun changing her clothing. Speechless, he frowned at her back.

She said, "We'll need to go to the boats soon." A moment later she murmured, "Kahl-maus. His despair is coming through our bond."

Needing to prove that he was not controlled, Joseph ordered her, "Block him,"

She shook her head.

His voice rose as he accused, "You're feeling sorry for that child-monster who killed you--and killed me just because you liked me? We're dead, Avianna! We're walking corpses whose families mourned us without having bodies to bury. My sister prayed over an empty grave for thirty-seven freakin' years!" His voice lowered, but cut the air: "Now, there are people in my family wandering as ravenous and rotted zombies, because I wasn't there to protect them. Don't you dare feel guilty over anything you did to Kahl-maus!"

"*Per favore, amore mio.* I have not forgotten or forgiven what he did to you, and I weep for your sister's agonies: but think. His sire turned and abandoned him when he was young and already a victim of his natural father's cruelty. That gives me a thin thread of *compassione.*"

"I don't care. He may have other creations out there."

"His loneliness runs so deep that I do not believe he has anyone else."

"Will you have Keenu reverse the spell?"

She shook her head and said, "*Mai,* no! I would never do that. He would do great damage again." She turned her head toward the western border and said, "Listen! The swampbuggies are leaving." Then she stared to the south and said, "The airboats are waiting for us."

It only took seconds for the vampires to dress in their hooded, ninja-style clothing and to arrive at the boats: Avianna and Joseph boarded together, Akio and Isamu boarded the second boat, with Ulric in the third, and Keenu in the fourth. Each of their crafts carried a small contingent of Marines. The boats followed their guides to the farthest reach of their search zone.

Around the tree trunks, the water reflected deep green shadows but, in the center of the channel, the surface reflected blue sky. The wind kicked up by the boat's huge fans ruffled the witch's long curls and everyone's clothing. The motors, like swarms of angry hornets, kept everyone except the vampires from hearing the natural world.

The pilots searched tributaries for biters. The Marines used binoculars while the vampires relied on their vision and hearing; none found anything unnatural. Large alligators followed between the wakes of the different boats.

Joseph leaned close to Avianna and said, "The alligators are so accustomed to human flesh that it will not be safe for people to return to the Everglades until the alligator population is thinned."

Avianna nodded and probed the minds of the Marines around her. From Kowolski's mind, she pulled memories of his hunting alligators in South Carolina. She made eye-contact with the Marine and held his gaze. Into his thoughts she infused the certainty that the alligators had come to attack the boats.

Kowolski signaled his pilot to slow down.

As alligators glided alongside the airboat, Kowolski placed a shot behind one of their eyes.

Marines in the other boats ducked, and scanned for trouble. Seeing the dead gator, they glared at Kowolski who waved his right arm in the chopping motion to signal his boat to speed ahead of the feeding frenzy he had triggered.

Joseph's eyebrows arched.

Avianna whispered, "*tu dici, io sì.*"

He shrugged.

"You say; I do."

Joseph smiled.

By midday the sun's pounding the canvas roofs that protected the vampires began to steam the air beneath them and perspire the humans. The pilots pulled the boats into the shade of overhanging trees. The Marines and witch opened the coolers that contained their rations and the five vampires left the boats to hunt zombies.

Chapter 28

Hunting

The vampires passed a group of wild hogs with their piglets. Not wanting to create orphans or kill the young, they left the animals alone. A solitary boar rooting among shrubs caught their attention.

Joseph said, "Avianna, that one might be over six-hundred pounds. We should bring fresh meat back to camp for the Marines."

Akio interjected, "Isamu and I can help."

"We are supposed to be hunting zombies," Henry complained.

Avianna glared at him and said, "Help or not.."

Henry frowned but drew his sword.

The vampires surrounded the snorting boar. The animal charged the nearest hunter, Akio, who leapt away. Panting and grunting, the boar lunged at Henry. Like a matador, the vampire side-stepped and drove his saber into the back crease of the boar's front shoulder. The beast roared and swung his tusks to the side, slicing open Henry's leg.

Henry went down screaming under the hooves.

Isamu rushed forward and drove his Katana into the boar's heart. The animal shrieked and stumbled, then fell with a ground-vibrating thud.

Akio helped Henry to his feet, and Joseph examined the crippling six-inch tear through thigh muscle. Joseph ripped the sleeve from the injured vampire's arm to make a tourniquet. He asked Akio, "Can you bring a med-kit from the boats?"

The samurai left before Joseph finished his sentence and reappeared with the kit.

"The cuts and bruises from the trampling are already healing," Joseph told his patient, "but I need to stitch the larger wound."

Isamu touched his brother's shoulder and said, "We will check the area for biters."

Soon after Joseph stitched Henry's leg, Isamu reported back, "We found none."

The samurai twins lifted the boar, and Akio grunted, "It is closer to seven-hundred pounds. We will bring it back to the boats."

Joseph stood and added, "I'll go with you in case you're attacked." He gave Avianna a sheepish smile that said, 'I know you don't want to, but,' and asked, "Would you stay with Ulric? He'll be able to walk soon but not yet."

"*Sì.* I will stay with **Henry**."

Joseph followed the samurai, protecting their flanks and backs as they carried the boar.

To the wounded man, Avianna said, "We have not seen a zombie all day. If all the units around the world find fewer biters, we supernaturals will have to prepare."

"To fight each other."

"No, my over-anxious foe, but for humans to attack us."

Blood loss grayed his skin and the features of his thin, angular face sharpened as he groaned, "They'll wait until they no longer see rotters."

"Then, they will remember to be afraid of us."

"But my fight is with you, Avianna. Linett was my child and I felt every bite, every shredding, every slow moment of her extreme agony. I felt her wounds as though they were mine . . . right up until the horde decapitated her."

Lost in sickening memories, Avianna did not respond.

Tears filled Henry's eyes as he asked, "Have you ever thought that the intimacy of the sire bond made her more my daughter than Keenu's?" Without waiting for an answer, he shouted, "What? No sarcasm? No wisecracks? No insults? No flirting? Do you finally understand why your existence is an insult to her memory?"

She whispered, "*Sì.* I have always felt it so."

Joseph appeared and announced, "Akio and Isamu are securing the boar to a guide boat. The crew will take it back to camp, but my patient needs to return with them."

With Joseph's support, Henry rose, saying, "I will need only a day or two to heal."

Avianna nodded.

The boat with the boar and Henry sped toward camp while the guides led the Marine convoy along different waterways. Gabriel shouted to his crew, "Where the hell are all the rotters?"

Shaking his head, Caleb grumbled, "With so many zombies gone, the alligators look leaner."

The pilots received both the order to return to camp and the information that the swampbuggy patrol did not find any zombies.

Later, after the boats were unloaded, Avianna asked Joseph to walk with her. She led him to a rarely used walkway along the marsh side and whispered, "I need to tell you something about Henry."

He gave a slight head shake then stared at her.

"Henry was Linett's sire," she said. Touching a finger to his lips to stop questions, she added, "and he has not forgiven me for bringing her to Dohiyi and not saving her."

"How long have you known? Why didn't you tell me?"

"Henry's need to avenge Linett has nothing to do with our promise to help the Marines."

"Would you really placate him with a fight?"

She took Joseph's hands in hers and insisted, "He is not wrong, *il mio amore*. He sired her. Then, I let the zombies end her."

"To save me! You came to me! His revenge should be on me."

She kissed his hands and said, "Every time you are injured or frightened, I feel it. Linett's destruction inflicted her anguish and pain on Henry. He feels her loss keenly—more deeply than we can and I did that to him, Joseph."

"What if you had saved Linett instead of me?"

"Then I would own your destruction instead of hers. Neither of you had the skill or strength for that battle. I owe Henry his challenge."

"No! You were not responsible for any of our choices"

"*Sì!* I was."

"So, now you risk my being destroyed with you."

Avianna kissed him then murmured, "Still, I must do this. Come back to our tent with me."

"You reminded me that sires can compel their progeny—that you can compel me. So, unless you are going to make me come to our tent, I'm going to the hospital to check on Shea. I assume you'll allow it!" He pulled his hands from hers and left in a blur of anger and speed.

Chapter 29

Backfire

Near midnight, a helicopter landed outside camp. A clean-shaven man wearing an Armani suit disembarked. He showed his papers to the guards and they opened the gate for him. Once inside, a Marine asked him to state his business. The stranger flashed a Homeland Security badge and insisted, "Classified."

"Where can I direct you?"

Saying, "I know where I'm going," the newcomer walked away. Turning a corner, he pulled a map from his jacket, examined it, and found his way to Keenu's tent. Hearing voices inside, he unbuttoned his jacket and drew his weapon.

A woman called, "Come in."

Inside, two women sat at a table with a lit candle between them. The petite and slender older woman wore a black and red gown with a high collar. She matched the photo he had of his target. Seeing the younger woman in a light floral dress, he thought, 'Collateral."

He attempted to fire, but nothing happened.

He struggled to ask, 'What?' but did not make a sound.

The older woman asked, "Legs a tad weak? Unable to use the gun because you already dropped it? You should sit before you fall."

The younger woman placed a chair behind him and eased the man into it.

"Intending to kill me, you must know that I am Keenu Kulae O'Mallory and a member of the International Council of Witches. What you may or may not know is that this is my daughter, Alexandria."

She glided to a side table and poured a golden-brown liquid from a pitcher into two empty mason jars. The witch touched the jars and they frosted. She handed one to Alexandria and said, "Sweet tea."

The two women sipped the tea, and the witch murmured, "Perfect." Then she smiled at her prisoner and explained, "White witches are Wiccans who are born or evolve more power than their sisters. White witches like me are symbiotic with nature. White witches, like my daughter, glimpse the future. None of us commit ritualistic murders or burn upside-down crosses. None of us deserve having SRD assassins—like you—come after us.

"I did say, didn't I, that my daughter has glimpses of the future? She knew all of you were coming for council members, so I warned the others."

Frowning, Keenu cupped her hand to her ear and said, "Too bad you can't hear that. It's the sound of the other twelve assassins, falling on their asses."

"Because I'm not there to help them sit," Alexandria interjected.

Keenu continued, "Ours is a three-part spell: defensive, compensatory, and secure. In our defense, each assassin falls asleep and stays asleep until his or her target dies of natural causes." To her daughter she smiled and said, "Is it unseemly that I am enjoying the explanation?"

Straight-faced, Alexandria answered, "A little, but he can bear it."

The assassin's eyes teared.

Keenu sighed and said, "Ah, you can weep—that's interesting; but yours and the other assassins' minds will slow. As compensation, computers have made it easier for us to flow every assassin's financial resources into his or her target's accounts. Bless your heart, the moment you accepted the assignment, you're bank account and the auctioning of all your possessions set up a trust for Alexandria to return to college.

"For our future security, assassins who outlive their targets will awaken without their memories; however, if any target dies **unnaturally** her assassin will stay asleep until a preexisting illness or age kills them. Reads a bit like a legal contract, doesn't it?"

Alexandria interrupted, "His eyes have closed, Mamma. He's unconscious. What now?"

From the entrance, Avianna said, "I am what happens now." Wearing the black ninja clothing she used for swamp patrols, she picked up the stranger by his waist band and dangled him like a garbage bag.

Keenu said, "Thank you, Miss Avianna."

"*Si. I nostri nemici ci rendono amici*; our enemies make us friends."

After the vampire left, Alexandria asked, "Mama, what's she going to do with him?"

Keenu raised her hand, closed her eyes, and intoned,

Sweet Mother of day and night, hide
Avianna from unwelcome sight.
Cast on her all shade—no light.
Help her to do what's needed and right.

After that expenditure of energy, she sat and sipped her tea before answering, "He's headed to a small Mexican village where a witch will secure him in a safe and remote place."

"But Mama, this is dark magic—again! Hilanor keeps warning you not to use it."

"The council, as one entity, cast the spell. No individual will carry the weight of it."

Alexandria frowned and stopped pushing for answers she might not want.

ttt

An hour later, in her tent with Joseph, Avianna laughed and said, "We vampires lack imagination. We drink our enemies dry: *cosi tedioso*. These witches are more creative."

He asked, "What did they do?" Then, his hazel eyes glimmered and narrowed, and he asked, "And, what did you do?"

"I mesmerized the assassin's pilot and crew. They believe he directed them to fly to the coordinates Keenu gave me. Then, they will believe he ordered them back to Washington without him."

"An assassin! The SRD sent an assassin?"

"*Si.*"

"What's Keenu up to, Avianna?"

She moved toward him, saying, "*Non lo so*: I do not know. Nor do I care. That is witch business. My business is in your arms for the rest of the night."

He backed away. In an edgy voice, he said, "Avianna, The humans are justified! They should be afraid of us! A werewolf killed a human child. Now, a witch cast a spell on an SRD operative—and you are complicit in his disappearance. We do what we want, whenever we want, to whomever we want—and that is terrifying! I need to stop being a part of it. I want to leave. I want to go to our ranch in Italy or our mountain retreat in Greece and stay there until every war everywhere is over."

Avianna straightened to her full height. Glaring at him she said, "You are the one who insisted on coming! You wanted to help our friends in the Marines. You wanted to help Keenu, and Mary and Kristian. You wanted to fight alongside Akio and Isamu, and to help your country— your country, Joseph, not mine."

"And now, I want to leave."

"And now, I don't."

They stopped speaking and, closing their minds to each other, slept with their backs to each other. The next morning, still silent, they left with the patrols.

Over the next three days, the warriors on the boats and swambuggies returned without finding a single zombie. At night, the Marines and supernaturals sat around campfires in small groups for quiet conversation. A private from the communications group played his guitar and sang.

On the third evening, with the sun low in the sky, the Lieutenant approached the still hooded vampires where they sat around a fire. The werewolves lie among them. Ritt cleared his throat and said, "I need to speak to Avianna, alone."

She stood and asked, "Shall we walk, Lieutenant?" They reached the end of a walk and, lowering her hood, she said, "Dawn and dusk are my favorite times. I love this. The sun having slipped below the horizon and the sky becoming cobalt blue."

"Avianna, Homeland Security contacted me about an agent who came here then disappeared."

"Should I care?"

Lieutenant Ritt's eyes narrowed as he said, "This is serious, Avianna. The crew reported that the agent diverted them to Mexico City before ordering the crew to fly back to Washington without him, but Mexico City International Airport does not have a record of the plane's landing there." Harsh and raspy, he asked, "Miss Avianna, did you have anything to do with this?"

"Why did he come here?"

"That's classified."

"Did you know about it?"

"That's classified, too."

"*Ovviamente*: Of course, you knew nothing. Why would you think I know more?"

"Because you could make him disappear and make his crew forget what happened."

"Lieutenant, did you not say that the agent left here, alive, on his own plane, with his own crew? Now, Sweet Lieutenant, this is not vampyr business, and I am still trying to make peace with my lover, so I will see you tomorrow."

An alligator floated through the channel without leaving a ripple. Neither the pale moonlight on the water, nor the alligator's serenity helped to calm Ritt's nerves. Shaking his head, he went to find the witch.

He found her in the galley with her family and Akio. Keenu moved wisps of Martin's blond hair off his forehead, and he smiled.

The Lieutenant decided not to question her in front of her family. Instead, he grabbed a sandwich to eat on the way to the hospital to visit Shea. The beautiful young woman was scheduled for transport to the hospital in Dohiyi for rehabilitation with her prosthesis. She had tried to convince him to come with her, but he was military to his core. He had tried to convince her to bring her brother and live on base with him, but she was a born and bred mountain girl. All that was left to him, was to keep her company for the time they had left.

ttt

In the galley, the O'Mallory family had just finished dinner when Alexandria paled and trembled. She turned to her mother and said, "I'm sorry, Papa, but I need to speak to Mama alone."

Kissing his daughter's cheek Martin said, "Okay, Darlin.' I'll turn in." Giving his wife a gentle kiss, he said, "I'll see you in a few minutes." He led Johanna and Akio out of the galley while his wife and daughter slid closer together.

Keenu turned to her youngest and snapped, "What, now?"

Alexandria whispered, "I had a vision, Mama. The Marines are going to break camp, but they'll want to take all the supernaturals back to their base. You and I will escape, Mama. The vampires will leave; but Kristian and Mary's pack—even with werewolf speed—cannot outrun the military."

"When will this happen?"

"You need to change the werewolves back into human form tonight or tomorrow."

Keenu patted her daughter's hand and whispered, "Okay. Go tell the wolves. It's going to take black magic, so I'll ask Hilanor and call my coven to ground me."

The two women rose, hugged each other tightly, and left the galley.

Chapter 30

Honor Bound

Late in the afternoon, Keenu and Alexandria entered the command tent. Already seated were the Sergeants, Girl, representing the wolves, and Avianna in a long-hooded cape. Lieutenant Ritt waited for the mother and daughter to sit before announcing, "I've just received orders to return to our home base and to leave any remaining zombies to the locals."

Creole Vanyan, in his first meeting as a Sergeant, said, "We'd like to visit what's left of our families."

"We'll return to base first, Sergeant. Then I'll arrange a leave rotation." Stressing the word 'invited,' he said to the supernaturals, "Y'all are invited to come back with us."

Keenu and Girl glanced at each other. Avianna gave a slight shake of her head.

Ritt continued, "Washington's been monitoring the increase in civilian hostilities toward supernaturals. Every headline makes people more fearful. We want to shelter the supernaturals who helped us and can only do that on base."

As wide-eyed and pixyish as a Margaret Keane painting, Girl said, "We werewolves have a community. There are families and friends waiting for us."

The Lieutenant, gentle but firm, answered, "We're asking the werewolves to stay wolves and scout for us on our way home."

The teenager started to speak, but a glance from the witch silenced her.

Avianna smiled and said, "Ah, *Grazia*, my friend, but your kind intention is *non è necessario*. We vampyr have places to go."

Ritt added, "Anytime there's a new outbreak or local authorities lose control of an area, we hope you'll deploy with us. That'll be easier from on our base."

Henry, in a short, hooded cape, lifted the tent flap and stood in the opening. "I heard everything," he said, "and it means Avianna and I have a date."

Avianna rose saying, "*Sì.*"

"The heliport area is large enough."

"Large enough for what?" Ritt asked.

Avianna hissed: "No, Henry. Our business is private—not performance art. *Nessuna discussione! Capisce?*"

Henry frowned.

Ritt cut in with, "Avianna?"

"Personal, Lieutenant. Let us go, Henry."

"Call me Ulric!"

Keenu interjected, "I don't know what's going on, but can you trust Ulric that his nest isn't waiting for you?"

"*Sì.* He has honor."

The two vampires left with everyone else still seated and unsure what to do.

Ritt spoke first: "In the morning, we break camp. I would appreciate supernaturals' leaving the room while I discuss procedure with my people."

In the swamp, Avianna led Henry toward the field where she had destroyed Kahl-maus's Adam and Eve. Two alligators lay in their path with lifted heads and open maws. The vampires took to the trees to climb over them. Then, they descended and leapt from root to root through a copse of mangroves.

Blocked by a wide channel, Avianna and Henry waded side-by-side through its thigh-deep water to reach the dry stretch of land on the other side. The sky darkened and the vampires lowered their hoods and lifted their faces toward the rising moon and emerging stars.

"You have never asked me not to do this," Henry murmured.

"Your anger is justified."

Remembering something he'd heard, he asked, "Was your father really your first kill?"

She walked without responding.

"At least tell me why you brought Linett into that battle. She'd only been a vampire for three years. You must have known she'd perish."

The older vampire, thought about how much or little she wanted to share. Then she answered, "I have never wanted dominion over another being, so I do not exercise my control over Joseph. I loved Linett but would not make choices for her." She hesitated before asking, "Why did you turn her? Why her?"

He stopped under a branch on which two warblers chirped and trilled. His eyes closed, and his angular features softened. Barely above a whisper, he answered, "I heard the lilting tones of her flute before I saw her. She sat alone on a park bench just before dawn, playing Debussy's 'Syrinx.' The half-light made a halo of her long, blonde hair. We played our flutes together for as long as I dared stay. Then I immortalized her. I preserved her delicate face and form, and her ethereal music." He made eye contact with the much older woman who appeared Linett's age. Henry added, "I would have treasured her forever, but she rejected the brutality of our existence and ran. Then you found her and let the zombies destroy her."

Avianna rested a gentle hand on his forearm. She did not remind him she and Joseph had traveled the world with Linett before the zombie infection—that they had helped the girl experience wonders she had not imagined. Instead, she said, "One of us will soon perish for your honor. Those we sired will perish with us, so tell me why you have more *compassione* for the lost Linett than for the others in your nest?"

"My other children make perfect but soulless music. Linett's gift came through her from heaven."

"You know, of course, that I will fight for Joseph's survival."

The dignified Civil War veteran replied, "My dear, I expect nothing less of you."

They made their way through tall grass before parting to wade through chest-deep water. They met on a dry hammock. A bobcat cried. A little farther ahead, a white-tailed deer leapt away, and an owl hooted high in a cypress.

Continuing, Avianna stepped around an orb-weaver's large web while Henry moved a branch, not to dislodge the toxic Lubber grasshopper resting there. A congregation of alligators roared in the distance and a colony of bats dipped and soared above them. A red wolf made a long and soulful howl.

Avianna smiled. Her Neapolitan accent thickened when she murmured, "I saw a red wolf yesterday. They have returned to the Everglades, these children of the night."

Henry laughed and added, "No vampire story is complete without them."

The two emerged into the open field where Avianna had fought her blood-siblings. The portions of the lawn that Adam and Eve had been burned struggled to return.

Henry assessed the field without comment. As he and Avianna moved twenty feet apart and faced each other, he quipped, "I wish I had one of my horses for a proper charge."

"I would never bring my horses here. They need larger fields and dry air."

"In case I am the one who perishes with my nest, Avianna, my horses will need to be saved. I have ten handsome Morgans near our cavern. Their location is in a portfolio in my tent."

"If I survive, Henry, I will send someone to help them. If I perish, my horses are at my *palazzo* in Italy: Akhal Tekes, Chestnut Andalusians, pinto Irish Cobs, white Camarillos; black Frisians, and Gypsies." She sighed and added, "*Bellissimo,* and well-loved by their caretakers."

"Caretakers?"

"I have protected the nearest village since the French king, Charles VIII, invaded Naples in 1494. I never hunted the villagers, and two of the local families have thrived behind my walls ever since. They are as loyal as humans can be, and I have left documents for them to inherit the estate and horses. Akio and Isamu are the only ones who know the location of my retreat in Thessaly, Greece—and the only ones, beside Joseph and myself, that the bats will allow near it. The retreat will belong to the samurai. Here in Florida we use a lovely rental. There is nothing to be done with it."

Henry drew his Civil War officer's sword and eyed Avianna as she unsheathed her Katana. Raising his blade to a middle position, he stepped forward.

Avianna raised her katana above her head and waited.

With a guttural yell, Henry charged her.

Avianna swiped downward at his weapon, knocking his blade to the side with the flat of hers.

Henry grunted and spun to come at her other side.

Avianna shifted position, making an upward sweep that blocked his sword. She waited with her blade ready.

He lowered his weapon for an upward swing.

Relying on battlefield experience and driven by revenge, Henry charged repeatedly and relentlessly.

Reluctant to kill him, but determined to survive, Avianna defended against one skillful and powerful blow after another. She advanced often enough to stop him from realizing she held back. That strategy cost her, and he drew blood.

Ulric held up his hand and said, "Bind your wound, Avianna. I do not want you bleeding out before I've destroyed you."

She tore a strip from her cape and wrapped her side; then they resumed. Through the darkness, metal clanged and flashed against metal without either warrior surrendering or tiring.

A haze of light on the horizon warned them of a rising sun. With new urgency, Henry lunged, slashing downward from his left.

Avianna deflected and spun around behind him. Off-balance, his powerful thrust carried him forward, and Avianna drove her free hand into his back. She grabbed his heart and crushed it in her hand, and then she withdrew it without taking his heart.

He turned to face her—but she had glided out of reach. Staring at her bloody hand, his mind blocked the finality of what had happened. Blood cascaded down his back and his limbs trembled. He dropped his weapon and sunk to his knees.

Avianna sheathed her katana and cradled him as he fell. On the ground, she guided his head to her lap.

He whispered, "Why didn't you rip out my heart and finish me?"

"I am not eager to return so honorable a man to the dust."

He strained to say, "I preserved the most talented musicians." As his skin dried and grayed, his strength faded. He rallied and added, "I wanted their music to last forever, but their harmonies and killing were all done with ice in their veins." He pushed out the words, "Now, I hear them crying, as they perish with me."

Avianna moved his platinum hair out of his eyes and murmured, "Ulric. I will forever listen for the sound of your flute on the wind."

Deteriorating, he murmured, "Henry."

Avianna reached into his chest and eased his heart out of it returning him to dust. Then she stood and sheathed his weapons and her own. Without brushing his dust off her clothing, she pointed toward the sky and the bats descended. They swooped close to the ground and swirled the air then spiraled upward. Henry's dust lifted from the grass and Avianna's clothing into the sky. She watched until there was nothing left to see. Then, she began her long walk back to Joseph.

She had not gone far before the sun crested the horizon. She stopped, not wanting to go farther or talk to anyone. She trusted Joseph to know that, because he existed, she existed. Finding a majestic hardwood tree, she stopped. She shredded saw-palmetto and carried it into the thickest part of the tree to make a sheltered nest. The length of her existence had made her more metaphysical than physical, preserving her even when she thirsted.

Surrounded by the breathing, melodic landscape of the Everglades, Avianna snuggled against the trunk. Later, she would return to camp and risk confessing hidden truths to the witch, but first, she slept.

Chapter 31

Doing Right

At twilight, Avianna woke and made her way toward the main camp. She mesmerized a doe and took only enough blood to sustain herself. Then she found a buck and did the same. Strengthened, she left both animals healthy and unafraid.

A human form came into view at the camp perimeter. The young woman said, "Miss Avianna."

"Alexandria. I am on my way to see your mother."

"Good. You need to tell her that Ulric is the one who killed my sister."

"How long have you known?"

Alexandria hugged herself. Her eyes closed for a moment before she admitted, "The first time I heard that you and Ulric planned to fight, A vision hit me—a vision of Ulric murdering my sister." Her brows furrowed as she remembered, "I don't think Linett suspected that the sophisticated man sitting beside her would take her life."

"Yet, you did not tell your mother."

The heavyset girl with a wreath of brown curls opened her eyes and stopped hugging herself. Straightening her back, she said, "I wanted both people responsible for my sister's death to fight each other. I wanted Mama to face only the survivor."

Avianna said nothing.

The two women, centuries apart in years and experience, appeared similar in age. In silence, they made their way to Keenu's tent. Reluctant to face the witch they had both deceived, they hesitated before entering.

Inside the tent, Alexandria and Avianna found Keenu, Martin, and Johanna sitting on two of the four cots. The seer frowned and said, "Miss Avianna has something to tell you."

Martin, always a gentleman, stood.

As the vampire stepped into the small space, Keenu said, "I'm not surprised or sorry that you're the one who survived."

"All of you need to hear what I must say, but I would prefer to discuss this outside under the stars."

The sadness in the vampire's voice prompted Keenu to ask, "Do you have something to tell us that we won't want to hear?"

"*Sì.*"

Martin pushed his blond hair away from his tired eyes and said, "Let's go outside."

The witch's family and the vampire made their way to a wide intersection of walkways. While the canal waters lay as still as a painting, the surroundings were alive with sound and movement.

Without zombies to eat, an alligator scrutinized the five people beyond his reach.

"This is far enough," Keenu said.

Johanna and Alexandria stopped, each one on a different side of their father. Alexandria, knowing what would come, hooked her arm under his.

The witch and the taller vampire faced each other. Heavily accented, Avianna murmured, "I came to tell you who killed Linett."

Knees weakening, Martin gasped.

Johanna placed a comforting hand on her father's back.

Keenu grumbled, "In Dohiyi, you said you didn't know."

"In Dohiyi, I did not know. I found out just before I came to the Everglades, but I had reasons to withhold it: your family blamed me for Linett's destruction, as I blamed myself. Her sire also blamed me, and he had both the right and the need to fight me."

Keenu spat, "The right? He killed my daughter—turned my daughter—and he had more rights than me—or Martin?"

"*Dai al diavolo il dovuto*: Give the Devil his due."

Keenu's anger stirred the air and a wind whipped everyone's hair and clothing. The water rippled and the gator snapped at the air. Tears streamed down the witch's face as she raged, "You let me protect that monster during the fighting here?"

Dark clouds churned above them. Horizontal rain drove through the screening and soaked everyone under the roof. The alligator slipped under the rolling surface of the canal.

Making no excuses, Avianna waited. Her pant legs and shirt sleeves flapped and her long, wet hair lashed her face.

Martin's daughters held onto him while gripping the railing with their free hands.

Martin pulled away from his girls and staggered to his wife's side. Wrapping his arms around Keenu, he blocked her view of Avianna. He kissed Keenu's forehead and neck, and then he shouted above the rattling metal roofing and tearing screens: "I love you! I am here for you. We can endure this together." He kept kissing her face and whispering his love until the rain stopped.

The dark clouds dissipated revealing a bright crescent moon. The alligator rose to the surface and eyed the people on the walkway.

As Martin led Keenu away, Alexandria and Johanna stayed with the vampire.

Avianna had always avoided Linett's twin and her identical hair, eyes, and willowy frame. Now, Avianna touched Johanna's thoughts and found a swirl of grief, anger, loneliness, and fatigue. Yet, under all that, Avianna discovered an autonomy and strength that Linett had never possessed.

Alexandria began to speak.

Johanna cut her off, saying to Avianna, "I found a YouTube video from before the zombies. It was Linett playing her violin on a concert stage in Europe and you were in the wings. Did you compel her to fight in Dohiyi?"

"No."

"Then I can't blame you for what happened there."

"Johanna!" her sister protested.

Tears trickled down the older sister's cheeks as she faced her sibling and insisted "Alexandria, Ulric turned Linett against her will, but Linett chose to stay away from home—away from us! She chose to be with Miss Avianna, and she chose to fight in Dohiyi."

"It destroyed her, Johanna!"

"Remember when you and Missy crossed North Carolina, through zombie-infested territories? Should I have blamed Missy if you had died?" Turning back to the vampire, she said, "You must have loved my sister very much to face Mama this way." She shook her head and said, "I have someone I need to see," then she turned and left.

Frowning at Avianna, Alexandria said, "I don't know what to say to you, but I need to see Mama." On the last word, she left as abruptly as her sister had.

She rushed to her parents' tent where she found her father resting. Worried, she asked, "Are you okay?"

"Yes."

"I don't believe you. With Mama tricked into protecting Linett's killer, neither of you can be okay. I'm sorry to have to leave you like this, because Mama needs to help the werewolves, and we are running out of time."

Keeping his eyes closed, he assured her: "Your mama already went to help them."

Alexandria kissed his forehead then left to find her mother.

Chapter 32

Agonies

Alexandria found Keenu and Hilanor at the heliport, lighting a ring of candles around the four werewolves. Outside the ring, Girl bit her trembling lip and hugged the rough military blankets she carried. Her scraggly, light brown hair hung in her hazel eyes.

"Kneel with us," Keenu said to Alexandria.

Alexandria knelt between the witch and the wizard and studied the wolves.

The white alpha, Kristian stood calm and steady, while his mate shot nervous glances at the humans. The huge black wolf, Jamaica, glared at the humans with unwavering intensity.

Alexandria met his eyes and trembled with desire. Then she forced her attention toward her mother. Never having helped the coven with black magic, she closed her eyes and searched her mind for the connection to her mother. She pushed past her oneness until she received a psychic tug from the coven sisterhood, followed by another, and another until she felt as one with the sisterhood.

The Wiccans in their village absorbed vitality from the natural world around them. They shared that energy with each other and with the young seer and syphoned their combined energies into their witch.

Alexandria's perception of the world intensified. The white wolves glowed under a bright fragment of moon. The silver strands in Elderwolf's gray hair flickered with light. The brightness of Jamaica's eyes kept the black wolf from merging with the darkness around them. Beyond the wolves, the songs of the frogs became distinct one from another, crickets chirped, cicadas buzzed, plants rustled. All of it pulsed within the young seer.

Keenu, anchored and strengthened by the others, cast the spell to reverse the lock she had placed on the werewolves' forms:

God of sun and moon and all,
Return the wolves to Lycan law,
And break the bind of hand to claw.
Return them to their truest state,
Bound to moon and lost to fate.

The witch, wizard, seer, and Wiccans flowed their collective wills into the werewolves. Any hesitation might leave the wolves half-changed and kill them.

Inside the circle, the wolves writhed in bone-cracking agony. Their howls scaled their tonal range then twisted into human screams.

As they lay naked and shivering, Girl ran and covered them with blankets. The werewolves tightened the blankets around themselves and helped each other to their feet. Unable to replace the warmth of their lost fur, they huddled together.

Hilanor leaned on his staff.

Alexandria helped her mother stand.

The haggard and weakened witch breathed unevenly.

As the first light of the sun glowed on the horizon, Kristian and Mary stumbled toward the witch and wizard. Kristian, rasped, "We cannot thank you enough for changing us back."

Mary added, "We promise you, as alphas, that you will be safe from us for as long as we are safe from you."

As the alphas spoke with her mother, Alexandria made her way to Jamaica.

Poised and regal, he had the same dark complexion as her mother, but his eyes glowed with an eerie light.

Alexandria breathed the name, "Jamaica."

"Alexandria, thank you for helping me communicate with my son."

"After you see Jaylan," she said with a smile, "you can invite me for breakfast—in the werewolf community, maybe?"

Exhausted, Jamaica murmured, "I'm sorry, Alexandria, but I need time with my boy."

Before the disappointed girl could agree, Martin and Missy ran from behind a helicopter and Missy embraced Alexandria.

Martin wrapped his arms around Keenu and led her away.

As everyone else made their ways back to their tents, Jamaica returned to his and found Jaylan half-buried under the covers and sleeping. The father pulled on a pair of jeans and a shirt. Then he sat on the edge of the cot and touched his son's hair.

Jaylan opened his eyes to see the man who had been lying to him since the orphanage. The eleven-year-old pushed the covers away and sat upright, saying, "Even when you claimed to be his twin, you seemed more like Dad." He dug into his jeans pocket and pulled out a wallet-sized photo, wrapped in plastic. He handed it to Jamaica saying, "Mom gave this to me. . . before the end."

Jamaica examined the photo of himself, his wife, and their four-year-old boy and said, "I remember when we had this taken. There should also be a larger, framed copy."

"It might have burned in the apartment. After healthy people evacuated, the army torched Cincinnati to wipe out the zombies."

Smiling at the photo, Jamaica said, "I'm glad you saved this one." After returning the photo, he reached into his pocket and pulled out a weathered and crumpled match. He showed it to Jaylan. "I kept my copy too," he said. He wanted to hug his son—but feared a well-deserved rejection, so he added, "I can't fix my leaving. I can't fix what happened to your Mom and you. So, where does that leave us?"

Jaylan stared at his father's crinkled copy. In a trembling voice he said, "I don't know." After a deep breath he added, "Maybe we start from here—but I don't want to live in a cave with wolves."

"No," Jamaica assured him, "It isn't like that. We're human most of the time and we own hundreds of acres in the Blue Ridge Mountains. Other werewolves have found their way to us and we've built cabins around a beautiful little lake."

"I have more questions."

"I'll answer them."

Jaylan fumbled with the words before saying, "Maybe it could work."

"Then we should pack. We're all leaving soon."

Before they could say more, Shea called from outside, "Jaylan, can you come with me? I need help."

Inside the tent, the boy did not move.

"Please, Jaylan."

He wavered, reluctant to go with someone who had kept his father's secret from him. Then, remembering why the one-armed girl might need help, he left his tent and followed her to the farthest walkway.

Shea took a deep breath and said, "A helicopter's waiting to take me to Dohiyi. So, I need to know if you and I are going to say goodbye with you still angry at me."

"Everything's been such a mess for so long that I don't know what I feel."

"I'm sorry I didn't tell you the little I knew about your daddy. The people we've lost, the killing we've done—I'm all mixed up, too." She touched her bandaged stump, and added, "And it's not a video game; we don't get do-overs. It's so—."

"Fucked up?" he finished the sentence for her. Remembering that she had lost her parents and sister, he said, "You're going home to your brother?"

"Yes. I hoped Lieutenant Ritt would come with me, but that can't happen yet. He's what my meemaw would have called a 'raht good man'—and that's why he can't leave the Marines." She touched the boy's shoulder. When he didn't pull away, she asked. "Are you going with the Marines to their base?"

"Can't say."

"I'm glad you have your daddy. We were in Dohiyi together and he is a fearless man. But, Jaylan, if you want to see me, Jamaica knows where Dohiyi is."

They leaned toward each other as though they would hug, but the boy pulled back.

Shea gave him a soft, sad smile, and they separated. While Jaylan returned to the werewolf tents, Shea went to the hospital tent and packed her duffle bag. Then she lay down for a quick and needed nap.

In his tent, Ritt packed his belongings.

From the open tent flap, an unfamiliar voice said, "Lieutenant," and Ritt looked up. There stood the guide boat pilot who had accepted Shea as a crew member.

"Yes?"

"Gabriel here. I jus' wanna tell you I bin talkin' to the locals. When the zombie infection done hit the reservations, the Seminoles and Miccosukee survivors built villages in the 'glades."

"They're not in my reports."

"Oh, they ain't showin' themselves to no armies. Tribal leaders jus' talk to a few of us locals. What I'm sayin' is—once y'all leave—we won't need no National Guard or police in here. The tribes and we locals will keep the place clean. If'n we can't keep it peaceful we'll give y'all a call."

Ritt smiled and shook his head. "The surviving police are spread so thin they might be happy to leave the 'glades to you people, but they'll want assurances that you'll be vaccinated."

"That vaccination thing might be a tall order for the tribes, but I'll ask their chiefs. Right now, I need to see Shea. What a little firecracker she is!"

"Yes, she is. I'll be seeing her off in a little while. She'll be headed home."

"You know, Lieutenant, she doesn't need two arms to do right by you."

Ritt blushed as Gabriel laughed all the way out the door.

Chapter 33

Slipping Away

Avianna's movements woke Joseph, and he whispered, "Where have you been?"

"I had to help someone. I wanted to see you before I do anything else."

"I trust you, Avianna, but I don't like your secrecy. It's wrong that I only know you're safe because I'm not dust."

"There are larger problems here than your hurt feelings—no matter how justified."

"You're reducing this to hurt feelings!"

"*Mi dispiace.* Tonight, Keenu restored the wolves to their human forms. Then, I mesmerized the flight crew and pilot that is taking Shea home. They will not see or hear that Alexandria, Jaylan, and the werewolves are on board."

"You did that while I slept?"

She eased her slender form into his strong arms. She kissed him and murmured, "*Per fervore, amora mia.* Set aside your anger and understand that I do what I must. Joseph, would you change me if you could?"

He pulled away, saying, "I want to return to our Florida home and my work at the research facility. I might be able to help find a cure."

"The government will look there. Keenu and I have been discussing other possibilities."

"Oh! And have you and Keenu discussed other possibilities for Akio and Isamu, too? Or do you only treat me as helpless?"

"Akio is in love with Johanna, so the brothers will go with the witch's family. I cannot keep arguing, my love, because I need to see the

Lieutenant. I promise to return to this *discussione* as soon as I am able."
She left him with his brewing anger.

Outside Ritt's tent, Avianna paused to listen.

Inside, someone announced, "I'm sorry, Lieutenant. We searched the camp for the source of those human screams but only found a ring of melted candles by the heliport. We can't find the werewolves anywhere, and their personal belongings are gone, too."

"Get me Keenu Kulae, and then check on the vampires and report back."

As the Private left, Avianna slipped into the tent.

Ritt stood with his back to her.

Avianna took a moment to appreciate the man she admired. With his cobalt blue eyes, light blond hair, and surfer-boy looks, Ritt was handsome; but Avianna had learned that it was his Mensa-level intelligence and courage that appealed to her more. As he turned, she purred, "Will you settle for me, Lieutenant?"

Hiding that she had startled him, he said, "Did the witch help the werewolves leave?"

"I will not say."

"Newspapers are blaming supernaturals for every missing child and serial killings in recorded history. Just live on the base until the media hysteria burns out."

"It will not burn out, Lieutenant, because we are not innocent. The media will always find small truths to magnify, and people will forget that we helped save them."

Sipping his coffee, he reasoned, "Then live on base because refusing looks suspicious."

"And, when Coraggio is given silver bullets to use on the werewolves, Kowolski is told to assassinate Keenu, and you receive orders to remove my head? *Quando conflitto*—when there's a conflict between honor and duty, what will you do?"

Ritt's expression tightened as he insisted, "Now that people know you exist, they'll never stop hunting you."

Her green eyes glowed as she sneered, "No one has hunted the samurai or me and lived. Predators after the wolves will become prey. Keenu should never be threatened."

"Avianna . . ."

"Do you know that China has opened her borders to all supernaturals? She has passed laws that punish humans who harm us, and she is ordering her people to accept us into their society. When China is thirty percent supernatural, she will be undefeatable."

Ritt frowned and asked, "Would you betray our country?"

"You forget, my sweet Lieutenant, that I am Neapolitan and my homes have been in Italy and Greece for more than eight centuries. I am only a visitor in the rest of the world."

"And Joseph? He's American."

"Even for my Joseph, today's crises will be tomorrow's history."

Ritt did not smile.

Handing him the portfolio she found in Henry's tent, she said, "There are creatures you can save, Lieutenant—Henry's Morgans are the best horses of their breed. They will be perfect for the calvary."

He took the portfolio and read the name 'Henry Gull' etched into its leather. He glanced up to find Avianna already gone. Shaking his head, he put the portfolio on his desk and went in search of Keenu. He found her at the end of longest walkway. She stared at the water while carpenters took down roofs and screening.

Ritt asked the workers to take a break, and they left.

"You need something, Lieutenant?" Keenu asked.

"You changed the werewolves back into human form, against my instructions."

Brows arched, she said, "You can find your way back to base without the wolves scouting for you; so, are you here to arrest me?"

"No one who lives on base with us will be a prisoner. Will you come?"

"You already know my answer."

Shaking his head, he left without a backward glance.

Keenu waited for him to disappear around a corner. Then she descended the ladder to the lower platform. There, in the shadow of the raised walkway, three canoes waited—each one paddled by two Seminoles. One boat carried Keenu and Martin. Another carried Johanna and Akio. The third carried Isamu.

Keenu asked the brothers, "Are you sure about coming?"

Akio whispered, "I am sure."

"I go with my brother," Isamu added.

Johanna nodded, "Mama, we have to hurry or we'll be caught."

Keenu gestured to the Seminoles to continue.

Staying in the shadows along the canal embankment, the canoes pushed through tall, pink, Muhly grass and wove around the thick trunks of cypress trees. Once they left the canal for open water, they glided forward.

Keenu said to her husband, "I have one thing I must do to shield Avianna and Joseph's escape." To the Seminoles she said, "Don't be afraid."

She closed her eyes. With arms extended upward, palms toward the sky, she intoned,

Black clouds swirl and thunder roar.
Lightning flash and hard rains pour.
Wind drive spying eyes indoors
To see departing friends no more.

Dark clouds churned. Thunder clapped and streaks of lightning met bolts rising from the ground. The rain fell hard, then harder, hammering the Everglades.

A Private, dripping water but shivering more from nerves than chill, ran to the samurais' tent. Not finding them, he rushed to Avianna's. He rapped on the pole and yelled above the storm, "Begging your pardon, Dr. Joseph and Miss Avianna, the Lieutenant wanted me to make sure y'all have what you need, but the samurai aren't there."

Avianna answered, "The samurai are with Keenu. *E stiamo bene.*"

"We're fine," Joseph translated.

The vampires listened to the Private leaving. Even through the storm they heard everything happening in camp. Avianna said to Joseph, "Clouds hide the sun. I will be able to bring the car to the bend in the road unseen."

He opened the tent flap, and she stepped out. As she transformed, he looked away. Then her high pitched and rapid chirps called to him.

Wet fur and drenched wings made it harder for other bats to fly, but Avianna powered through the storm.

Back in the tent, Joseph rolled Avianna's mattress bag containing a thin layer of her native soil. Then he folded her ungainly dresses and his jeans and shirts. He shoved everything into duffle bags and finished just as he heard the Bentley's approach.

Guards pulled their hoods close to their faces. No one saw Joseph dart through the storm. Dressed in black and carrying the heavy bags as though they were weightless. He leapt over a railing and into the marsh below. He dodged an alligator and ducked under a dangling snake. A minute later, he and his duffle bags were soaking the inside of the Bentley. He leaned back and said, "Avianna, let's just go."

Wearing the sandals and simple dress she kept in the trunk for after transformations, she drove through the tempest. Each in their own thoughts, they did not talk. A little over an hour later, they pulled up to a dock just north of Homestead.

There, they found their two boats waiting: a sixty-foot long, gaff-rigged schooner named *Day Dream,* and a thirty-eight foot sailboat, named *Little Dream.* Both had white painted surfaces with polished teak woodwork, and sky-blue fabrics and sails. The entire time the vampires were in Florida, a team of craftsman and a contingent of guards, refitted, redecorated, and protected their boats.

Joseph boarded the sailboat to check on his supply of frozen cow's blood.

Avianna compelled the workers to give bags of blood for her schooner's refrigerator. She faced two problems. First, chilled fresh blood lasted only forty-two days, while she did not know how long she would be at sea. Second, they could not freeze fresh blood because it would crystallize without the process that blood banks and hospitals used.

The rain stopped and the sky cleared. Before the work crew left for home, Joseph gave them his Bentley to sell. Then Avianna entered their minds to replace all memories of her, Joseph, and their boats with false memories. After the crew dispersed, Avianna boarded the *Day Dream* and Joseph boarded the *Little Dream.* They sailed under a clear twilight sky.

In camp, the wizard, Hilanor approached Ritt in the galley and asked, "May I join you, Lieutenant?"

"Of course."

"You're frowning."

"That witch and her storm covered almost all the escapes."

"Almost?"

"You're still here, Hilanor. Why?"

"Alexandria said for me to tell you and Captain Nicci when he arrives."

"Nicci's coming?"

"Yes, but for now, I want hot coffee and warm food. Shall we dine together?"

Ritt nodded and spent the following hours smiling through the wizard's story-telling, while his failure to contain the supernaturals gnawed on his nerves.

The next morning, Nicci arrived to find Ritt waiting for him. In his late thirties, the tall and wiry Captain, rubbed his haggard face. Brown hair poked out of his helmet. His olive complexion had paled, and his amber eyes had lost their sparkle. Seeing his Lieutenant's expression, the Captain blurted out, "What the hell, John! Here too?"

"What do you mean 'Here too'?"

"In the past forty-eight hours, military camps world-wide, have reported the disappearance of their supernaturals."

"In every camp?"

"Vampires, werewolves, witches, wizards—they all seemed to evaporate."

The officers passed soldiers and staff packing the last of the gear. In the command tent, Ritt poured hot coffee for them and said, "They're all gone. except Hilanor. He said he'll only tell us why, together. I had no reason to detain the human reporter, Missy, so she took a bus this morning."

"Lieutenant, have you heard that China is offering the supernaturals sanctuary? The new worry is that they'll turn them into an army"

"China's not hiding her invitation, and North Korea is a new rumor."

Hilanor opened the tent flap, saying, "Excuse me, gentlemen. May I join you?"

Nicci pulled over a chair for the centenarian, and Ritt handed him a cup of coffee. The wizard's hundred-plus years had etched into his face. Nicci asked, "Why are you still here?"

"To go home with you, Captain."

"Back to base?"

"No, to your home. Alexandria said that you'll see your family before reporting to base and that I should go with you . . . to live out my last years there. She says the aroma of your mother's tomato sauce came through her visions. She also said I should call it gravy."

Nicci cocked his head and asked, "Why would you want to end your life with my family?"

The wizard shrugged and explained, "Alexandria saw me laughing with your grandmother, playing chess with someone, and eating at a long table filled with loving people."

Nodding, Nicci said, "It's hard to argue with that girl's visions. Are you packed?"

"Yes."

"Okay, grab your gear and meet me at the T-wall." To the Lieutenant, he said, "You and I have to file reports with Washington about the supernaturals' departure. After I leave, finish breaking camp and keep me apprised of your progress."

When Nicci reached the T-wall, Hilanor was waiting. The elderly wizard carried a cloth bag and leaned on the staff made from the limb of an African Blackwood tree—a gift from Avianna.

Nicci smiled and said, "I guess I'm inviting you to come home with me, but I have to check on my other outposts first."

Hilanor nodded, and they boarded the Captain's armored vehicle. While the driver took them out the gate, the gunner on top of the AFV searched for zombies without finding any.

Hilanor leaned back and closed his eyes. He thought about Missy and Shea back in their homes, and Alexandria, with Jaylan, and the werewolves in the Blue Ridge Mountains. He visualized Keenu and Martin with Johanna and the samurai in the Wiccans' village. Then he imagined Avianna and Joseph sailing toward the coordinates Keenu had given them. The wizened old man breathed easy and slipped into a peaceful sleep.

For the next twelve days, Avianna and Joseph piloted their spell-bound ships toward Keenu's coordinates. When the boats reached an area between the Caribbean and the African coasts and between the northern shipping lanes and the cruise ship lanes to the south, the vampires anchored and waited.

Chapter 34

The Birth of a Sanctuary

In the Everglades treehouse village, Keenu and the coven spent the early morning on the walkways. They touched dew-kissed leaves and inhaled sweet floral scents.

At noon, the witch and Wiccans entered the meeting room and lit a circle of candles. Keenu sat in a lotus position. Two women placed a wide and heavy glass bowl in front of her. In the bowl, soil, sand, and shells lay under sea water. Two toy boats floated on the surface. Within the ring of candles, the sisterhood sat and joined hands.

Keenu closed her eyes, stroked Merlin, and envisioned Avianna and Joseph.

The phone rang and it was Avianna saying, "We're ready. Joseph anchored the *Little Dream*, and he is on the *Day Dream* with me."

"Say the words I taught you."

Through the phone the witch heard the vampire say, "Let it be here; let it be now."

Keenu hung up and extended her hands over the bowl. Turning her palms down, she began,

Mother of land and sky, and Father of seas:
God of creatures all.
Protect them from what will be--
Changes large and small.

Below the vampires' schooner, all sea life capable of swimming or scurrying away fled the epicenter of the spell. Currents carried away the slower creatures.

Keenu contemplated the contents of the bowl in front of her. Focusing, she intoned,

Heat and power of the core
Reshape this land forevermore.
Raise toward heaven a new, safe place,
Slow and steady, movement with grace.

Below both the real and the toy boats, the earth rumbled, and roiling lava pushed upward. Sand and shells slid down the rising mountains.

The witch pulled energy from the Wiccans, and everything in the bowl and in the sea responded to her will. She held her hands above the bowl and intoned,

God of all and Earth Mother fair,
Raise this mountain to the air.
Higher and higher from its base,
Toward the skies, show its face.

On the *Day Dream,* the vampires clung to the railings and each other as the schooner pitched and shuddered. Around them, craggy peaks broke through the sea's churning surface, lifting their boat.

When the upward movement stopped, earth and rock shifted with a deafening roar, forming a cavern around, under, and above the *Day Dream.*

Trembling, Joseph whispered, "Keenu is terrifying."

Pointing toward a gap in the cave wall, Avianna shouted, "We have to run for that opening."

Together, they dropped over the side of the boat onto the moving rocks below it. Dodging falling debris, they leapt from one shifting boulder to another until they reached the opening. They stumbled through a short tunnel and emerged on a beach that had formed around the base of the mountains. Seared by the sun, they yanked their hoods over their faces and tugged their long sleeves over their hands.

In the meeting room, Keenu pulled more strength from her sisterhood. Then she touched one fingertip to the bare crags of earth that poked above the water in the bowl and whispered,

Cool from without and from within.
Allow the earth to be a skin.
No more turmoil, no more rise.
It's time to rest beneath the sky.

In the bowl and on the island, the earth quieted. Where tsunamis should have risen, only gentle ripples touched the shores. The smaller boat bobbed unharmed offshore.

Keenu sipped water from a glass. Then she raised her arms toward the ceiling, palms-upward, and continued,

Clouds roll in and darken all.

Onto this land, the rain must fall.

Keenu trickled water from a drinking glass down the sides of the new peaks. The water filled and overflowed the island's depressions and cracks, creating waterfalls, pools, and rivers.

Pale and shaky, the witch said, "We can eat and rest. Then, we'll continue."

On the island, winds slowed and a steady rain fell. "Let's look around," Joseph said. The two walked under a heavy cloud-cover until they found a large pool. The lovers slipped out of their clothing and into the water.

Avianna closed her eyes but Joseph said. "We need to talk."

She opened her eyes.

"When you met me, I was a physician and, in all ways, a man. I was independent and self-sufficient. Now, you treat me like a child that you need to protect. I resent it more with each passing year!"

Not wanting to appear seductive, she lowered herself in the water to cover her bare breasts. "Joseph," she began, "I loved and traveled with Hilanor for almost fifty years and fought beside the samurai for a little longer. In seven hundred-plus years that's over two-hundred and fifty-five t-h-o-u-s-a-n-d cold and loveless nights."

Though he did not move toward her or speak, his expression softened.

Avianna continued, "Then I met and befriended your sister, and you walked into my life. I fell deeply and completely in love with you—the doctor and the man. Loving you so, I still did not kill you to keep you with me."

"But you turned me."

"Yes—after Kahl-maus killed you. Yes, I selfishly, urgently, turned you and I protect your existence because I never again want to walk this earth without you."

Joseph closed his eyes. He remembered seeing her for the first time and the music of her first hello. He allowed his love to flood his mind and flow into hers.

They stayed in the water, silent and physically apart, but eternally bound.

When the horizon brightened, they left the pool. They dressed and strolled toward their cavern.

In the Wiccan village, Keenu dragged herself to her home and to her waiting husband. She dropped onto the bed and fell asleep before Martin had time to question her. He kissed her forehead, pulled a sheet over her, and ate a portion of the dinner he had made for them.

The next morning, Keenu woke and had coffee and a pond apple. Then she rang the gong for the sisterhood to return to the meeting room.

Each carried a hollowed gourd holding different seeds than the others. Kneeling within the circle of candles, they closed their eyes and touched their leader's spirit with their own. Keenu stretched her arms, palms upward, over the water and earth bowl and murmured,

Float on breezes; sail on seas:
Grasses, flowers, fruits, as seeds.
Come to this bare, waiting land.
Nest then rise through soil and sand.

From the dish beside her, the witch took seeds, and sprinkled them over the formations in the bowl. Each of the other woman did the same.

Carried on the wind, seeds settled in new and moistened soil. Coconuts floated toward the island's shores.

When the coven sisters finished, Keenu rose and said, "Rest and have lunch. I'll sound the gong when it's time to return."

After sharing the noon meal with Martin, the witch summoned her sisters to regroup. Within the circle of candles, they held hands and stared at the seeds spread over the brown earth and rocks. Keenu murmured an incantation that encouraged the seeds to take root. When she finished, the sisterhood repeated her words as a chant. Then Keenu said,, "Sisters, thank you for your trust and for all you have done."

On the island, seedlings reached through the soil. Crabs laid their eggs in the sand. Fish darted under seaweed in the shallows. Joseph, shook his head and said, "It's wrong for anyone to have this much power."

"There can't be many in the world who can do this—maybe there's only one."

"What comes next?'"

"You and I need sleep. Later, we can bring the sat-comm from the ship and secure it on a mountain, so I can contact Keenu." She surveyed the landscape around them and added, "After the plants and trees have grown, we will sail to the nearest islands to bring wildlife back here."

He nodded and led her through the cavern tunnel to the undamaged and secure schooner. Inside their cabin, their bed waited for them; under it lay two zippered bags of soil: one from Naples, Italy, and the other from Joseph's birthplace. The vampires slipped into bed and slept away the daylight hours.

That night, they set up the sat-comm, and Avianna contacted the witch. "Keenu," she said, "I am forever in your debt. If ever you need me, I will come."

Keenu answered, "Just pledge yourself to my daughters. If they need you, come."

"I pledge myself to both your daughters."

"Avianna, I never thought I would forgive your for tampering with Alexandria's mind—for making her forget seeing Linett's death. Now, I'm grateful."

"I hear fatigue in your voice, my friend. You need sleep. *Buonanotte amica mia.*"

After they ended the call, Avianna and Joseph explored the island again. Already seeing seedling sprouts, they walked for hours.

They returned to the cavern while soft streams of light still filtered through cracks in the earth. Undressing for bed, Joseph frowned and said, "But is this it? Do we hide here while a war breaks out between supernaturals and humans?"

"You heard me promise my help. I keep my promises."

"Avianna, you and Keenu planned this island without considering that I don't want to hide anymore."

She touched his cheek and kissed his hand, "*Sii paziente.*"

"Be patient?"

"I have killed good people and I need to stop—before I become even less human than I already am."

"Your terminating zombies gave peace to the dead."

"Yes, but no peace came from killing Adam, Eve, and Henry. There is no possible peace from letting Linett perish. Please, my love, believe that

I could become a monster you would not want to know—one you would stop loving."

He kissed her and stroked her hair. "I'm sorry," he whispered, "We'll stay here until you trust yourself again."

Without words, they gave to each other all the passion and love they had to give. Afterward, they slept through the day while the world continued without them.

Their friends, supernatural and human, had already settled in separate sanctuaries hoping for a respite they did not believe would come.

Chapter 35

Finito

In the Wiccan's village, the samurai--cloaked against the sun—worked through the daylight hours to build their treehouse. Stopping when the residents needed to sleep, the vampires tried to rest through the night. This reverse of natural vampyr design, continued from the Marine camp, wearied them.

Different from the Wiccan's straight angles and solid walls, the brothers sculpted a roof with soft lines and curved eaves. Sturdy posts bore the structural weight, so paper walls could be moved to change the floor plan.

Akio had come to the Wiccan village for Joanna. Isamu had come for his brother. Johanna watched them work until she felt intrusive. Then she sat and dangled her feet over the edge of a walkway. She and Akio had grown so close that she imagined sharing the new house with him as her husband. An image of her twin, Linett chided her, "Yeah. Bring Mama and Papa a vampire son-in-law after one vampire killed me and another didn't save me." Johanna's brows furrowed, and she pressed her lips into a thin line. To clear her mind, she studied the scene below the walkway.

A pair of spoonbills used their large talons to anchor their thin legs to tree roots above the water. The birds held their green-tinted bald heads high, and their pink-crested wings glowed against the dark water.

Johanna thought about Alexandria, half a country away, gazing at the same sky. Their differences did not stop Johanna from missing her younger sister. She murmured, "I wish you'd stayed with us."

ttt

On the porch of their Blue Ridge Mountain cabin, Alexandria squeezed into one of two rocking chairs. Closing her eyes, she envisioned Johanna sitting on a treehouse walkway. "I miss you," Alexandria whispered, "and I miss Mama and Papa too." She inhaled the aromas of oak, red firs, and white lily and murmured, "But North Carolina—our first home—is still mine."

Girl, emerging from the cabin, asked, "Who are you talking to?"

"I'm musing."

Waif-like and wearing jeans and a white T-shirt, the young werewolf curled in the other rocking chair with room to spare. "Well," she said, "I gathered firewood and collected berries and herbs. We have nothing else to do besides wait for me to leave with the pack."

"What do y'all want me to do while you're hunting?"

"Your precognition saved us in the Everglades battles, so we'd like you to keep doing that. Oh, and if you're living here, you'll need to choose our side."

Alexandria tugged her yellow floral dress over her heavy knees and answered, "Missy and I are journalists. We stay neutral and report what happens."

"When humans and supernaturals kill each other, neutral may not be possible."

Alexandria hugged herself and said, "I can't see what's still changing."

Girl stood, leaving the chair to rock itself, and huffed, "Well, can you tell us when the war will start?"

Alexandria admitted, "There's no opening bell. It may have already started."

Girl snapped, "That's some useless power you have."

"You just said my second sight saved y'all!"

Jaylan stepped up onto the porch with a large dog beside him. The malamute was all white except for a black saddle. He limped on a bandaged left front foot. The boy studied the girls and asked, "What are you arguing about?"

As the dog sniffed at her, Girl backed up and asked, "Who's that?"

Jaylan stroked the dog's head saying, "Dad and I were chopping wood when Varg hobbled out of the forest with a cut on the bottom of his foot. Dad bandaged it."

"Varg?"

"That's what's on the name tag, but the sheriff said no one's reported a missing malamute, and the registry doesn't have that name. What did you say about Alexandria's power?"

Girl explained, "She can't see much about the coming war."

Jaylan asked, "I'm human, with a werewolf dad. What happens to us?"

Frowning, Alexandria answered, "I don't know."

ttt

Elderwolf sat on the porch swing of the cabin he shared with a widow. With his fatigue lingering after his Everglades wounds healed, he sagged onto the swing. Although his mix of wolf and human blood had slowed his aging, he had less speed and strength than younger wolves.

The widow emerged to hand him a steaming cup of coffee. He slid over and made room for her. Grey-haired and plain, she took the seat and smiled but said nothing. After zombies killed her human husband and their werewolf children, she lost the energy for extended conversation.

Holding the coffee with his right hand, Elderwolf rested his free hand on hers. Pointing toward Jamaica's cabin, he said, "See there? All that hammering will bring any zombie that's still out there straight to us."

"Jamaica needs a room for his son."

"But I want to be done with fighting."

"We won't be done until they're done: zombies, humans, whoever."

"Even though Alexandria saved us more than once in the 'glades, clairvoyants give me the willies." He stopped himself. Stroking her hand, he said, "Sorry I'm so grumpy. Let's just enjoy this peaceful day."

She squeezed his hand.

ttt

Almost three-hundred miles away, in a forest on the North Carolina piedmont, Captain Nicci sat at a table with his family and Hilanor. The old wizard sampled everything: warm garlic bread, home-made penne topped with thick red gravy, sausages and meatballs, egg-plant parmesan, and antipasto made with vegetables from the gardens.

Jim's grandmother waved at Hilanor and sang, *"Mangia, mangia, amico mio."*

Hilanor, having been intimate with Avianna's for fifty of his younger years, did not need a translation for the Italian invitation to eat.

Jim's mother, Elena—middle-aged with thick, dark hair and penetrating eyes—leaned close to the wizard and whispered, "The bloggers are talking about a war between the supernaturals and humans. *Dimmi*—tell me, why are you here? Are you the wolf among us sheep?"

Hilanor grinned. Every member of the Nicci family carried one kind of weapon or another. "I don't see any sheep, my dear," he answered, "and I have been sent by someone too guileless to plot against you."

Elena repeated, "So, why are you here?"

He breathed in the aromas of basil, parsley, and garlic and answered, "A very smart young lady told me I will know when the time comes." After dinner, the family played baseball while Hilanor cheered them along. At the same time, he evaluated their fortifications.

Noticing Hilanor staring at the walls, Nicci took a break from play and called to the wizard, "Let me show you around." The two walked along-side each other, with the Marine slowing his pace for the old man. The Captain explained, "When the infection spread, the uncle who owns this farm invited the extended family to live here. They built the wall while I was deployed."

Hilanor laughed and said, "It would keep out King Kong." He did not say the wall would not stop spells or vampires.

Nicci continued, "The forest around us is on government land, but they were too busy to notice that my uncle built the wall from a wide circle of their trees. That barren perimeter lets us see what's coming."

Nicci, pointing to a row of five-foot tall wooden barrels, explained, "They collect rain. Each one has a hose at the base that runs underground to irrigate a different garden. We also have three wells for our drinking water."

Hilanor peered into the nearest gardens and mused, "Corn, sweet potatoes, soybeans, peppers, lettuce, tomatoes . . . all thriving. Impressive."

"We have twenty-three adults here, and fourteen children all ages. That's a lot of hands and strong young backs. We also have an architect, a college professor, carpenters, and mechanics. One of my aunts is an oceanographer, so we enlarged the pond for her aquaculture. One of my cousins is the fluid dynamics engineer who redesigned our underground irrigation and all our plumbing."

Acrid smoke rose from the tall chimney of a nearby shed. As they passed it, Hilanor asked, "You have a forge?"

"We make bullets out of anything we can spare. We have wooden bullets for vampires, silver bullets for werewolves, and lead bullets for humans."

In a corralled field, fifteen mares ran with half a dozen foals. Hilanor stopped to admire them saying, "Beautiful."

"My uncle owned six adults. The family found the others on abandoned farms or running loose." Nicci paused before asking, "Why are you here?"

Hilanor sighed and said, "Alexandria would never send me to betray your family." Already tired, he worried that Alexandria might have sent him to protect the Nicci clan—something he might not be strong enough to do. "Perhaps," he added, "she only sent me here to enjoy eating, drinking, laughing, and resting with your wonderful family."

"Well then, do you play checkers?"

"Of course."

"Come with me. I think you should meet my uncle."

As the two men walked back to the main house, Hilanor stared southwest. Something stirred there: something menacing.

ttt

Unseen, Kahl-maus floated over Savannah, Georgia. Below him, Spanish moss draped from the widespread arms of oak trees. Unable to speak or to touch anyone, he searched for a telepathic connection. He descended to just above palmettos then wove around holly trees. He settled in a crepe myrtle to eavesdrop on a couple walking by. Their laughter intensified his loneliness. He rose again and continued his search.

Outside the city, his mind touched another with telepathic ability. The vampire dove out of the sky toward a cottage in the shadow of a tall magnolia. A heartbeat later, he swerved away from that same mind—one too strong for him to control. He fled that area and found a nook in which to hide through the daylight hours.

The following evening, he made his way to Charleston, South Carolina. Despairing, the cursed vampire pushed himself to continue. He probed the minds that passed under dogwoods and sweet bay. He needed a forlorn and isolated soul, one vulnerable to his control. Unless he found a new puppet, he could do little to shatter Avianna's peace.

The End